"Are you moping, or what?" Angie asked after getting a look at Sam's pensive face.

"I'm beginning to think Roni knows me pretty well," Sam answered. "I think I've been avoiding men too carefully."

Angie sat cross-legged on her bed. "This sounds interesting."

"Scott O'Connor was here today to talk about the article I wrote. I really liked him," Sam admitted. "But I've given it a lot of thought and decided I've been away from guys too long. Maybe *any* guy could have walked in here today and left me breathless."

"Maybe," Angie said.

Sam wished Angie had agreed with her more wholeheartedly. If it wasn't a matter of her wanting a man's company, then there had to be something special about Scott O'Connor. And knowing how unlikely it was that Scott was thinking about *her* right now, the last thing Sam needed was a one-sided crush on the Hawthorne Hawks' star center. She'd move straight from sophomore slump to sophomore dump.

Other books in the **ROOMMATES** series:

Roommates

NO CONTEST
Alison Blair

IVY BOOKS • NEW YORK

To the 1987 Minnesota Twins,
who won the World Series
the same day this book was finished.

Ivy Books
Published by Ballantine Books
Copyright © 1988 by Butterfield Press, Inc.

Produced by Butterfield Press, Inc.
133 Fifth Avenue
New York, New York 10003

Library of Congress Catalog Card Number: 87-92095

ISBN 0-8041-0088-8

Printed in Canada

First Edition: May 1988

NO CONTEST

Chapter 1

"Welcome home, Liz," Sam called from the suite's living room. She walked into Liz and Roni's bedroom and looked around. "Where's Roni?"

Liz pointed to a stack of cardboard boxes behind her that Roni was attempting to carry. "Happy New Year!" Roni drawled.

"You look like you're moving in all over again," Sam observed. "What is all this?"

"You won't believe what I got for Christmas!" Roni exclaimed. She dropped the pile of boxes on her bed and opened the top one.

"Ooh," Sam said when Roni pulled out a soft peach-colored cashmere sweater.

"And the best stuff isn't coming until tomorrow!" Roni announced.

"What?" Sam stood back with her hands on her

1

hips. "You got so many presents that you couldn't carry them all?"

"You've got it." Liz shrugged. "Roni couldn't fit everything in her car, so her mother's having the rack system shipped up here."

"Rack system?"

Liz explained, "You know . . . AM/FM tuner, amplifier, equalizer, turntable, double cassette deck, and CD player. State of the art, as they say in the stereo business. Every electronic thing invented so far!"

"Oh, is *that* all?" Sam joked, trying not to show how amazed she was by the extravagance of Roni's parents. "It sounds like you've actually seen the monster, Liz."

"I had dinner at Roni's house one night during vacation," Liz said, "and her dad set up the whole system to make sure it worked."

"Did it?" Sam asked.

"It sure did," Roni said with enthusiasm. "My parents almost fainted during the sound check. Hey, Sam, do you know anyone who would want to buy a used stereo? Cheap?"

"Well, what about Maddie and Stacy?" Sam knew they had a small cassette deck, but it was no match for Roni's slightly used stereo system.

"Do you think they'd like it?" Roni wondered aloud.

"Let's find out." Sam reached around the boxes on Roni's bed to find the phone. But before she could get to it, Stacy and Maddie ran into the room. "Welcome back!" everyone cried at once as they hugged each other, acting as if they'd been separated for months. "Maddie, how was your vacation?" Sam asked.

"You know what I did," Maddie told Sam.

"Sure, *I* was with you for New Year's, but these guys weren't anywhere near Chicago."

Maddie gave everyone an account of her last three weeks. She had attended several faculty holiday functions at the college where both of her parents were professors. And according to her, school looked a lot different—more fun, less panicky—from the teachers' point of view. Then Sam had come to visit her, and that's when they went to the "wild" New Year's Eve party. The only thing wild about the party was that it had been wildly boring. Sam and Maddie had left at exactly 12:05.

Stacy had met her family in Aspen and skied her entire vacation. Her tan face proved she'd spent plenty of time on the slopes. She said that her mother had finally stopped trying to convince her to transfer to a "more appropriate" college in New England.

"Is Angie back yet?" Liz wanted to know.

"She's in the room, unpacking a bunch of beads she brought back from California," Sam replied.

"Sounds like she's planning to get her jewelry career going again. I think I'll go see how she's doing." Liz went through the living room to find her friend.

"Hey, I almost forgot. Would you guys like my

stereo?" Roni turned to Maddie and Stacy.

"Like to do what with it?" Maddie asked.

"Oh, I don't know. You could use it as a table, I guess."

"She wants to give it to you guys!" Sam volunteered, knowing Roni would tease them forever if she had her way.

"But we already have one," Stacy reminded her roommate.

"Yeah, but it's not like Roni's," Maddie replied, eyeing the large speakers on the other side of the room. "Why don't you need it anymore?"

Roni grinned. "I just happened to get an all new system for Christmas!"

"Must be rough," Maddie moaned. "We'd be happy to take this old, outdated junk off your hands for you."

"Great. I'll let you know when my present arrives." Roni hung a new pair of black wool slacks in her closet and stretched out on her bed. "Well, I hope y'all had lots of fun over vacation, because tomorrow we have to get back to work. The party's over."

"It's not *that* bad," Maddie said. She was sitting in the chair at the foot of Roni's bed. "I'm going to try out for the play the drama department's producing."

"What are they going to do this semester?" Stacy asked.

"I'm not exactly sure, but it's a play written by a senior."

"That sounds interesting." Stacy shifted to get more comfortable on Liz's bed.

"I don't have anything in mind as exciting as starring in a play," Roni drawled. "But I did hang around the registration lines long enough to sign up for the physics section with the best-looking guys in it."

"I can see it now." Maddie laughed. "Roni's going to try on at least ten outfits tomorrow morning before she's ready to stroll into class at two o'clock!"

"I bet you're right," Stacy agreed.

"So what if I do?" Roni's eyes flashed. "A girl has to have goals."

"You can't argue with that," Stacy observed. "I'm looking forward to my art class. I've never really tried to paint before, and it's going to be fun seeing if I can do it."

"What about you, Sam?" Maddie asked. "You've been awfully quiet so far."

Sam leaned against the headboard on Liz's bed. "I've just got all the regular classes: nineteenth-century British literature, European history, child development, and . . . statistics. I wish I'd signed up for Roni's physics class, it sounds like fun."

"What's the matter?" Maddie said. "I thought you liked all those I'm-going-to-be-a-teacher-some-day classes."

"I do like them. It's just . . ." Sam couldn't quite explain how she felt. Last semester she'd been too busy. Her class load had been heavy, and she had exhausted herself with the effort of getting over Aaron Goldberg, her ex-boyfriend. She should be glad that her class schedule was easier, and that she could finally look at Aaron without getting a lump in her throat. But instead, she felt bored and restless.

"You don't sound very convincing," Stacy said bluntly.

"I know," Sam answered honestly. "There's nothing really wrong with my plans for this semester, but I just can't get excited about them."

"I know what it is," Roni said, a smug look on her face. "Sam's got sophomore slump."

"I've heard about that," Maddie said. "It strikes college sophomores every year, right? When they least suspect it . . ."

Roni laughed. "Yeah, that's it. Sophomores tend to get bummed out because nothing is as new and exciting as it was their freshman year."

"Freshman year *was* exciting," Sam admitted.

"For all of us," Maddie agreed. "But now Angie and Erica and the others are the new kids on the block, and we're supposed to be more . . . mature. We have to pursue our own interests, choose our majors, get more serious about the future."

"So why aren't I looking forward to my classes?" Sam asked them all. "They're all about my future. I've always wanted to be a teacher."

"Because you need a change," Roni explained. "And I've got just the answer. You need a new guy."

"Nick!" Maddie and Stacy called in unison.

"Please, not Nick." Sam smiled and shook her head. "If I were going to get the hots for good old Nick, it would have happened by now."

Roni nodded. "You're right. Nick's been after you since last summer, and you never really liked him. What kind of guy do you think you want to meet?"

Sam thought for a minute. In the past, the guys she'd gotten involved with had taken the first step. She hadn't picked them out of a crowd; they had chosen her. "I guess I'd like someone who's more exciting than Jon, but not as intense as Aaron. Another Jon would bore me to death, but I don't have enough energy to keep up with a guy like Aaron again."

"I'll see what I can do," Roni offered. "Maybe after I find Mr. Right in my physics class, there will be someone left over to fit your requirements."

"Roni, why do you always think a guy is the answer to everything?" Stacy asked with her arms crossed over her chest. "Personally, I think a new image might do the trick. I'll take you to the great hair salon I found in Atlanta and let them create a new Samantha Hill. That would pull you out of your slump!"

Sam played with her long, blond hair. "Thanks, but I don't think so. I'm kinda used to looking like this. Besides, looking different won't make me *feel* any different."

"Yeah." Stacy shrugged. "You're right about that."

"I know what would help," Maddie said quietly.

"Let us guess," Roni interrupted. "You think she should try out for the play, tutor someone, and join the Gold Key club."

"I'm not going to tell Sam what to do. But getting involved in campus activities can be really rewarding. You meet lots of people, you can make some new friends—"

"Male friends?" Roni inquired.

Maddie rolled her eyes. "Maybe, but even if she doesn't meet any guys, I'm sure there's something Sam could find to do that she'd enjoy more than her classes."

"Really, Maddie," Stacy said. "You think being active is the solution to everything."

"Well, it usually helps," Maddie claimed.

"I think Maddie's right," Sam finally said. "But what should I do? I can't even think of anything I'd want to try."

"Baby-sit faculty children? Join a health club? Help Angie with her recycling projects?" Stacy suggested.

Sam wasn't crazy about any of those ideas, but now that she thought about it, one thing she really liked to do was write. And she also liked people, and she enjoyed doing research. There must be someplace she could use those skills. Suddenly, Sam knew what she could do. "I've got it! I'm going to work for the *Hawthorne Herald*."

"The school paper?" Maddie said with a puzzled expression on her face. "What will you do for them?"

"I'll be a reporter. I'll write about campus activities, and I'll investigate any wrongdoings," Sam said dramatically.

"It sounds like you've been talking to Aaron, Hawthorne College's conscience," Stacy noted. "I thought you were over him."

"I am," Sam assured her. "But a few things about him rubbed off on me. I think I'll always care about the world since Aaron showed me one person *can* make a difference."

"The next thing we know, there will be a television crew on campus, profiling Sam Hill, ace reporter, muckraker, college sophomore," Stacy kidded.

On Monday afternoon, Sam was surprised to find the newspaper office buried in the dark, somewhat deserted basement of the Student Union. Travel posters and old *Herald* clippings covered the cement block walls. It didn't look as though any of the desks matched, but it didn't matter because stacks of papers and old pop cans covered most of the desks anyway. Considering the slick, well-respected newspaper the staff produced each week, the environment was completely out of sync.

"Who do I talk to about working for the paper?" Sam asked the first person she saw.

The guy slid his glasses down his nose to take a

closer look at her. "Are you here about the ad for a typist?"

"No, I want to be a reporter."

"Hey, Eddie!" the guy called over his shoulder. "This girl says she wants to be a reporter."

All around her, heads turned in Sam's direction, and she tried not to be embarrassed. A guy with medium brown hair walked toward her. "Hi, I'm Eddie Sawyer."

"Editor of the *Herald*?"

He smiled. "That's right. So why do you want to be a reporter?"

"I like to write, and I think there are a lot of interesting things happening on campus that should be covered," she explained. Sam could see he wasn't impressed by her reasons, but they were the best ones she had.

"Well, we have all the people we need to do the cute feature stories," he told her.

"I didn't come in to ask for a job like that," she explained. Not that she didn't read the cutesy pieces in the paper, but Sam didn't think they were what she wanted to write.

"Exactly what *did* you have in mind?" Eddie cocked his head and looked more closely at Sam.

"Um, investigative reporting," Sam ventured.

"Just like that? You think you can just walk in here and ask for one of the most prestigious positions on the staff?"

Sam stared at her loafers for a minute. It hadn't occurred to her that at the *Herald*, just as at major newspapers, people had to put in their time doing less glamorous jobs before they worked their way up to the exciting positions. She supposed she could do something else until she could prove to Eddie Sawyer that she'd be a great investigative reporter. "Well, what could I do if I can't do that?"

"I don't know. I'll have to look at a sample of your work. What do you have with you?" he asked.

"With me?" she repeated dumbly.

"Did you ever write for your local paper back home or for your high school paper?" he asked, helping her get his meaning.

"No," Sam admitted. "All I have are old term papers. You could read one of those if you wanted to."

He laughed. "No, thanks. Look, I don't usually do this, but we could use someone new in the staff room this semester. Would you do some test articles for me?"

"Sure." Sam couldn't believe her luck. It was well known around campus that Eddie Sawyer was very choosy about his staff, and he didn't give just anyone a break.

"I'd like you to do a piece on the girls' basketball game."

Stacy's suitemate Jean Jones was on the team, Sam remembered. Maybe she could help Sam with the article. "Sure, I'd be glad to write something up," Sam said enthusiastically.

"I'm not saying we'll use the story, but treat it as if it were your first assignment," he cautioned.

"Okay, no problem," Sam promised.

"And to see how versatile you are, I'd like you to check out the rumor that the seventies streaking fad is about to be revived at Hawthorne."

Sam smothered a giggle. "Streaking? As in naked people running around?"

He nodded. "Do you have a camera?"

Sam gulped. "No."

"I'd like a shot of the basketball team in practice—and anything or anyone else interesting you might discover," Eddie said with a grin. He pointed to a small girl sitting behind the front desk. "Check with Nancy. Tell her I said you could borrow one of the newspaper's cameras."

"Thanks! When do you want the stories?"

"They should be on my desk by three o'clock, Thursday afternoon." Sam blinked. "Is that too soon?"

"Oh no, not at all." Sam wasn't about to blow the opportunity he was offering her.

"Good. I hope your class schedule isn't too heavy, because if we use you on the staff you'll be living with a lot of tight deadlines."

"Sounds great. I'm definitely ready to get to work," Sam assured him with a shy smile.

Tuesday afternoon, Sam found her friends in Stacy and Maddie's room. "Hi, guys. What do you know about basketball?"

"I think it's the sport between the football and baseball seasons," Maddie said with a grin.

"All I know is, the players look great in those

cute little shorts. Well, at least most of them do."

"You're missing the point," Sam interrupted. " I need technical information on plays, strategies, stuff like that."

The girls looked at each other. "You've come to the wrong place," Maddie advised. "What's the deal?"

"The deal is I just spent the last two hours watching the girls' basketball team practice, for my first *Herald* assignment. I've watched hundreds of games, but when it came to being a serious observer, I realized I didn't have any idea what I was supposed to write about," Sam explained.

"So what are you going to do?" Roni asked. "Now that you know we're clueless."

"I guess I'll go to the library," Sam said, shrugging.

The others groaned. "You're taking this too seriously, Sam," Stacy said. "You don't need to know everything just to write one little article."

"Really," Maddie protested. "When I suggested getting involved, I didn't mean for you to get just as buried in work as you were last semester. Whether you're in the library for a class assignment or you're there for a newspaper article, you're still working alone."

Sam rocked back on her heels, surprised by her friends' concern. "This is only research for one article," she pointed out. "And if I do a good job on this I'll get a spot on the staff. Then I'll be interviewing people and getting all around campus on *Herald* business."

"Didn't you say you had two assignments?" Stacy asked.

"Yeah," Roni chimed in. "You said they gave you two topics, but you only told us about one. What's the mystery?"

Sam cleared her throat. "It's no mystery. My other article is supposed to be on streaking."

"Streaking!" Roni screamed. "As in naked men?"

"You've got it." Sam shook her head. "Eddie Sawyer, the *Herald* editor, says it's supposed to be a new fad on campus. What am I supposed to do? Go around asking guys if they're streakers?"

"That could be interesting," Maddie said with a sly smile.

"Wait a second," Stacy suddenly cried. "The girls at the Alpha Pi house were talking about this yesterday. There's a rumor the Pi Phi guys are going to streak in front of the Alpha house tomorrow night!"

Sam stared at Stacy. "You wouldn't be making this up just to make me feel better?"

Stacy put her right hand over her heart. "Scout's honor. It's just a rumor, but the girls at APA seemed to believe it."

"Well, then I'd better get to bed early tonight. I could be working late tomorrow," Sam said, relieved to have a lead on her second article.

"You're really dedicated," Maddie observed. "I think you'll make a great reporter. But have you given up your idea of being a teacher someday?"

"Are you trading in the screaming kids and chalky erasers for the recognition and glamor of the media?" Stacy asked dramatically.

Sam rubbed her sore behind. She had never noticed how rock-hard gymnasium bleachers could be. "The glamour of the media? I think that's just another rumor."

given up your idea of being a teacher someday?"

"Are you going in the morning," Vida and shaky except for the revolution," and Elinor in the medical," she asked dramatically.

She rubbed her sore behind. She had never noticed how much hard gymnastics. She better could be. The glamour of the medical labor that's just another lunch."

Chapter 2

Glamorous was not the word Sam would have used to describe her job at eleven o'clock on Wednesday night. She knew that January could be cold in Georgia, but the temperature had to be below freezing. It was bad enough that her fingers were almost frozen to the camera button, and her foggy breath was going to give away her hiding place. She had found a small, cleared spot behind the shrubbery in front of the Alpha Pi house and she was crouched behind a bush, trying not to let her teeth chatter.

It was close to eleven-thirty when she heard wild screams in the distance. Holding the camera carefully, she tried to figure out where the noise was coming from, just as four guys came into view on her right. Sam was just about to take her first picture when her hands started shaking. *Loosen up, Hill,* she told herself sternly.

The first naked guy had already run past by the time Sam got control of herself, but she managed to get a shot of the second guy from behind, and a much better picture of the third streaker.

"Hey, did you guys see a flash?" the third one yelled.

All four turned toward the bushes, and Sam suddenly realized she hadn't prepared an escape plan. What would she do if they found her? More important, what would they do? Pose? Or steal her camera? Sam didn't want to wait around to find out.

The bare branches scraped against Sam's legs and pricked through her jeans as she scurried along the side of the building, still hidden by the shrubbery. The guys were almost to her old hiding spot when she turned the corner and dashed at full speed away from the house.

Then, out of nowhere, her toe hit a tire and she fell, her right knee crashing against a bike on the ground. Although her first reaction was to sit for a minute and check whether or not her leg was bleeding, the thought of four naked guys made Sam jump to her feet. She sprinted as fast as she could toward Rogers House, not even bothering to limp until she reached the front steps.

"Home," she gasped, "at last." Sam ignored the curious stares directed toward her as she shuffled through the lobby and headed upstairs. She didn't care what people thought; she was too busy thinking about the nice, hot bubble bath she was going to take when she got to her room. Her feet were frozen and her leg was throbbing. Soaking in some steamy water would take care of both problems. Sam vaguely heard someone calling her name, but she was almost to her room so she kept walking and pretended she hadn't heard a thing.

"Sam!"

She turned around when the voice grew more insistent. Jean Jones was jogging down the hall toward her.

"I need to talk to you," Jean explained, catching her breath as she reached Sam.

"To me?"

"Yeah. I saw you at basketball practice yesterday," Jean said.

Sam pushed some hair out of her face. "I'm doing a brief story on it for the paper."

"Really? That's great." Jean stood quietly for a few seconds. "I, um, wanted to talk to you about the team."

Sam could see Jean was upset about something, but she was in no mood to offer advice or have a long chat in the hallway. Her leg hurt more and more as she stood on it. "Okay, but I'm really beat tonight. Could we do it later in the week?"

Jean took a close look at Sam as she bit her lip. "Yeah, sure. Later will be fine."

Sam heard the disappointment in the freshman's voice and she felt guilty for turning her away. "I promise we'll talk soon, Jean. If I don't find you, come looking for me."

Jean nodded. "Okay."

Eddie Sawyer sat back in his chair. "This is good stuff," he told Sam. She had dropped off her two stories and the roll of film early that morning. She was surprised he had taken the time to look over her work already.

"Did you get the film developed yet? Or don't I want to know?"

He grinned. "You haven't seen the pictures?"

"No, I just got here." She reminded him.

Eddie handed Sam some black-and-white glossies. The first two basketball shots were fuzzy; she'd been figuring out how to use the camera. The others were much better, and one actually captured Jean blocking a shot. The next picture showed the bare back of one of the streakers she had seen Wednesday night. And the other picture she'd gotten of one streaker was nothing less than embarrassing. Sam felt herself blush as she quickly handed the pictures back to Eddie.

"You'll understand if we don't use the streaker story and photographs?" he asked.

Sam laughed. "Even if you did, I wouldn't want a by-line. It was bad enough being chased by them."

"They chased you?" Eddie sounded surprised.

"They sure did," she told him. "And I have the wounds to prove it."

Sam started to pull up her pant leg to show him

the nasty scrape, but she thought better of it when he pushed back his chair and looked much too interested in what she was doing. She rolled her pant leg back down. "Really, it's nothing."

Eddie sank back into his chair. "If you say so."

"So, did you like my work?" she asked, anxious to turn the conversation away from her injury to the real reason she was standing in front of his desk.

"Yes, I did. Very much. In fact, I've got a place on the staff for you. Interested?"

"You bet!"

"It doesn't matter what the assignment is?" he asked, raising his eyebrows.

Maybe she should have taken the eyebrows as a warning, but Sam was determined to show Eddie Sawyer she wasn't some prima donna. Sam liked the idea of being a reporter. It didn't matter what kind of events they wanted her to cover. She would make the stories interesting and important in their own way.

"Hey, Mark!" Eddie yelled across the room. "Come and meet Sam Hill, your new reporter."

Sam turned in the general direction of Eddie's gaze. Her heart sank when she saw the guy coming toward her. It was the same one who had assumed she wanted to be a typist for the *Herald*.

"This is the Sam Hill you told me about?" he demanded of Eddie. "I was expecting someone bigger and taller . . . and male."

"You saw the story on the girls' basketball game and you liked it," Eddie reminded him.

"Sure, but I didn't know it was written by a girl."

Sam was beginning to get irritated. As if working for this male chauvinist wasn't bad enough, writing for the sports page was even worse than doing cute, little feature stories. "Excuse me, but are you the sports editor?"

"It's time for you two to meet," Eddie declared. "Sam, this is Mark Malone, the *Herald*'s sports editor. And Mark, this is Samantha Hill, your new reporter."

"Nice to meet you," she said, as politely as she could.

"Same here," Mark muttered.

"Why don't you take her over to your department and get to work?" Eddie asked. "You're the one who's been screaming for a body since Joe left campus on an internship for the semester."

Mark nodded toward another desk. "C'mon."

Apparently, Mark Malone couldn't deny she was a body, Sam mused as she followed him to a battle-scarred desk piled high with clippings, notes, and telephone messages.

His desk was apparently the entire sports department; there wasn't another desk or chair nearby. As he sat in his chair, she leaned on the right front corner of his desk and tried to look at ease.

"Joe, the guy who's not here, always did our 'athlete of the week' highlight. Think you can handle it?"

Sam pictured the sports section of the paper in

her head. Mark was talking about the column that always ran on the last page of the paper, detailing an amazing feat by a Hawthorne athlete. Faking more confidence than she felt, Sam said, "Sure. Who's supposed to be highlighted this week?"

Mark Malone rolled his eyes. "It's your column. You figure it out."

Sam nodded. "When do you need it?"

"By one o'clock on Saturday—at the latest."

He might as well have asked Sam to sit down and write it right away. It was Thursday afternoon; that gave her less than forty-eight hours to find a star athlete and write the column. Mark was definitely testing her.

"Something wrong?" he inquired when she didn't respond.

"I was just thinking, that's awfully soon," Sam said.

"That's life at the *Herald*." He shrugged. "All articles are due by one o'clock on Saturday so the paper can come out Monday morning."

"Sure." Sam felt silly for thinking that he was picking on her. Of course, the articles had to be submitted in time for them to be typeset and printed before Monday. "I'll have the article for you Saturday morning."

He cocked his head and gave her a look that said he'd believe her when she delivered it on time.

Sam stared back at him. "Anything else you need to tell me?"

"Nope."

"Then I think I'll start looking for my athlete of the week." Not giving him a chance to say anything else or give her another one of his strange looks, Sam turned and headed for the door. She had no idea where to look for her wonder athlete, but Mark Malone would never hear that from her lips.

Sam squeezed between Maddie and Roni on the bleacher seat and pulled a notebook out of her backpack.

"Are you really going to take *notes*?" Roni asked in disbelief.

"She has to do it for her article," Maddie explained.

"This is her last chance to find an athlete."

"Maddie, please." Sam opened her program to look at the team roster. "You make it sound like I'm looking for a boyfriend or something. This is just a job."

"Is it?" Stacy asked, sliding into the open spot on Maddie's other side. "I think you're working so hard because you want to impress someone at the *Herald* office."

Sam thought about Eddie Sawyer and Mark Malone. "Not the way *you* mean it," she told Stacy. "I want to prove to them a *girl* can do the work, but that's the extent of my interest in impressing the men I've met at the newspaper office."

"Are you sure?" Roni asked. "I thought Eddie

Sawyer wanted to see your legs."

Sam hoped no one else was listening to their conversation. "He wanted to see my *wound*, not my legs."

"Sounded like he really wanted to see that scrape you got when those streakers were chasing you," Roni commented gleefully. "Imagine if they'd caught you!"

"Roni, shh. People are listening," Sam said quietly. "Just drop it, okay?"

Roni sighed. "All right. But I hope you meet someone while you're working for the paper. Considering all the time you're putting in, you deserve some perks."

They all rose for the national anthem, and then the game started. The Hawthorne Hawks roared down the court to score first, and Sam was tempted to forget her assignment and cheer along with the crowd. But she didn't want to try explaining to Mark Malone that she couldn't find an athlete of the week because the game was too exciting for her to work during it. So she kept track of some of the best players and scribbled quick notes about the big plays, still trying to keep up with the hectic excitement of the game. It didn't take long for Sam to realize that the hero of the game was Scott O'Connor.

Scott always seemed to be in the right place at the right time. When a teammate passed him the ball, he was always in the perfect position under the basket. If he had the ball and couldn't get a shot off, he passed to a teammate who could.

Sam jumped to her feet with the rest of the crowd when Scott sank a dunk shot that put the Hawks ten points above the Newville Lions. She had barely taken her seat when he grabbed a rebound at the other end of the court and raced back to score again. Sam wondered if Scott O'Connor was always this dominating or whether this was his lucky night.

Sam was fascinated by Scott's moves. After her basic research on basketball techniques, she could tell he really knew what he was doing. And he wasn't bad to look at either, she admitted. He was tall, about six foot five, and he moved with such speed and grace that he outclassed everyone else on the court. His dark brown hair was short enough to keep out of his eyes, but he hadn't gone in for the crewcut that seemed so popular with other Hawthorne athletes. He was obviously a leader, not a follower. If Sam had to choose one word to describe Scott O'Connor, it would be *style*.

"Sam, you're almost drooling," Roni observed. "Is the game really all that good?"

"We're up by fifteen points. Of course the game's exciting enough to leave a sports reporter breathless," Maddie said logically.

Stacy leaned over to get a good look at Sam. "I don't think that's it, Maddie. She's kind of flushed. Maybe she's sick."

"Isn't he great?" Sam asked them all in a soft voice.

"*He*?" Roni could barely conceal her delight.

"It's happened! She's finally noticing a person of the opposite sex! Who is it?"

"Number Eight," Sam whispered. "He's amazing."

Three pairs of eyes fastened on Number Eight just as his hook shot gave the Hawks two more points.

"He's a hunk," Roni declared.

"Gorgeous," Stacy agreed.

"You guys have it all wrong," Sam told her friends. "I've been admiring his skills, not his body. I think he's playing a great game, good enough to be the athlete of the week."

"And that's all you've noticed?" Maddie asked. "Just the dunking and passing and stuff?"

"Of course. I'm here on business."

"Oh, how could we forget? It's so obvious." Maddie rolled her eyes and everyone laughed.

Sam couldn't tell if they thought she was too serious about her job on the paper, or if they really didn't believe her interest in Scott O'Connor was purely professional. She didn't bother to protest or try to set them straight. What did they know about objective reporting?

Chapter 3

Angie roared into Suite 3D and slammed the door behind her. Without a word, she threw her books on her desk and dropped onto her bed right on top of her favorite stuffed animal, Sparky the Seal.

"I know Mondays can be tough," Sam said, looking up from her desk. "This is a wild guess, but did something happen today?"

Angie jumped off her bed and started to pace around the room. "Do you think animals have rights?"

"Animals? What kind of animals?"

"Why should it matter?" Angie countered. "I mean, do you think some animals do but others don't?"

Sam shook her head and tried to figure out

what Angie was talking about. Was she intent on saving baby seals or whales? Was she upset about fur trappers? Had she been talking to people at the animal shelter in Hawthorne Springs? "You've lost me, Angie. What happened today?"

"The psychology department!"

"What about the psychology department?" Sam prompted.

Angie perched on the edge of Sam's bed. "They got a grant to study reactions to certain stimuli. But instead of using student volunteers, they're bringing in a dozen chimpanzees!"

As far as Sam knew, scientists experimented with chimps quite often. "They're a lot like people. Doesn't it make sense they would use monkeys?"

Angie couldn't have looked more shocked if Sam had said she thought nuclear warheads were safe. "You mean, it's okay to prod, poke, and poison them because they can't complain?"

"I didn't say that." Sam tried to collect her thoughts and defend herself. She hadn't slept much last night because she'd been so excited to see her first article in this morning's *Herald*. "I was just saying that there are reasons why scientists use chimps or monkeys or whatever."

"Yeah," Angie snorted. "The biggest reason is that people wouldn't let the experimenters do those things to them. So the scientists use helpless animals who can't complain. Someone has to speak up for those chimps."

"And you think you're the person who should

be their representative?" Sam asked, beginning to sense that Angie had a plan.

"Do you see anyone else volunteering?"

Sam gazed out the window at the students slowly walking back to their dorms after their Monday classes. "No."

"I think the best approach will be a protest, with a lot of people." Angie sounded as if she'd already given the matter much consideration. "I have to figure out how to do it, and fast."

"Don't you get tired of protecting nature and the environment all the time?" Sam asked.

"It can really interfere with my class work," Angie admitted. "But if you really care about something, you care all the time . . . not just when it's convenient."

Sam nodded. She'd spent enough time last year with Aaron Goldberg, self-appointed student activist, to know when it was pointless to argue. Angie couldn't turn her back on a cause any more than Aaron could. "Is there anything I can do?" Sam offered.

"As a matter of fact, yes." Angie answered so quickly that Sam knew her roommate had had something in mind all along. "An article in the *Herald* would advertise the problem to the whole campus."

"How can I help you with that?" Sam asked.

"You're on the staff," Angie said impatiently.

"I'm a *sports* reporter. I don't think I can slip a mention of the chimps into next week's article on a basketball game."

"I didn't mean you had to write it," she explained. "but you must know someone else who could cover the story."

"Not yet. With all the short deadlines, there isn't a lot of time to socialize in the office," Sam said. Also, until Mark Malone really accepted her as one of his sportswriters, Sam didn't want to look like the kind of person who hung out, chatting and gossiping all the time when there was work to be done.

"I see," Angie said curtly. "Well, if you get a chance . . ."

"Sure." Sam couldn't stand disappointing Angie. The California freshman was going to have a hard time campaigning for monkey rights, and Sam didn't want to make it more difficult. "If I have a chance to mention the story idea, I will."

"Thanks." Angie got back to her feet. "I think I'll go see if Tucker has any suggestions."

Sam tried to concentrate on her child development book after Angie disappeared, but she couldn't help trying to imagine what Tucker Morris III was going to say about Angie's desire to protect the monkeys. He would probably be more interested in how the psych department had managed to get the grant money. She shook her head. Angie and Tucker had to be the strangest couple on campus.

Three strong knocks on the door in the living room surprised Sam. She couldn't imagine who it was. Her friends usually walked right in when they wanted to see her, and she didn't know anyone who would knock so hard. She stood up and opened the door a crack, then peeked out.

She saw a shoulder. Looking higher she found a familiar face, but she couldn't quite believe it. She could be hallucinating, but she was pretty sure it was Scott O'Connor standing there.

"Hello?" Her voice was weak, and Sam realized her heart was beating out a crazy rhythm.

"Sam Hill?" he asked.

"Yes."

"May I come in?"

Sam tried to open the door wider and jammed it into her foot. Knowing she couldn't feel any more stupid or clumsy if she tried, she stood back to let him into the room. Scott was much taller and bigger than he had looked on the basketball court Friday night. He seemed to take up the entire room.

"Please, have a seat," Sam offered. She sat down on the couch, and gestured to a chair opposite her.

"I've got to talk to you about this article," Scott began in a deep, serious-sounding voice.

He handed her a copy of that day's *Herald*, folded open to Sam's column. His tone warned her he hadn't stopped by to pay her a compliment. "You didn't like being the athlete of the week?" she hazarded.

He leaned forward to rest his elbows on his knees. "Let's just say the guys on the team didn't think much of it. You made it sound like I won the game all by myself. I wasn't out there alone, you know."

Sam looked into his hazel eyes. He looked very honest, and he was obviously upset. She tried to make some sense out of his concerns. "The athlete of the week highlight is a usual feature in the *Herald*. Surely you're not the first basketball player to be profiled in the column."

"Of course not. But I might be the first to have been noticed when someone else deserved the honor."

Sam didn't believe the aggressive player who had charged down the court could be so modest. "Who deserved it then?" she asked.

"Jim Barker."

Who in the world was Jim Barker? Sam wasn't going to make a complete fool of herself and ask Scott O'Connor. She couldn't ignore the fact that he was every bit as gorgeous as Stacy and Roni had said he was. And it was just Sam's rotten luck to be alone with him and look this stupid.

"Jim Barker is a junior on the swim team who broke the conference record in the two hundred-meter butterfly by two full seconds," he explained.

Sam didn't see a hint of smugness in his fascinating eyes, although he had good reason to laugh at her. Not sure why she trusted him, she decided to abandon her tattered pride. "That happened last week?" she asked.

"Monday afternoon."

Monday was the day Sam had gone to the

Herald office to ask about a position. Now she knew why she hadn't heard about Jim Barker: She'd been too busy watching the girls' team practice free throws, not to mention staking out streakers. It was mostly her fault that she'd made such a big mistake and missed the big story, but Mark Malone could have given her a hint, at least.

"Have I lost you?" Scott inquired.

"I'm sorry." Sam realized she'd been rolling and unrolling the newspaper he'd handed her. She set it aside. "I do see your point, and it's embarrassing."

"You're not the only one who's embarrassed. You should have heard what the guys said when someone finally figured out that Sam Hill was actually Samantha!"

"Why is that so bad?" Sam was tired of people acting as if it were unnatural for her to be covering sports.

"They were already unhappy about the column, and when they found out it had been written by a girl . . ." He stopped and stared at his big feet. "Well, you can probably guess the reasons they came up with for why you would have written such a glowing review of my performance."

It was Sam's turn to stare at her feet. Her cheeks burned as she thought up the kinds of conclusions the guys must have made. "Maybe it's time for me to tell you what really happened." Sam sat back on the couch and hooked her thumbs in her jeans pockets. It was never easy to admit to being wrong, but she felt strangely comfortable with him.

"I only joined the *Herald* staff last Thursday. Apparently they were short one 'body', as they put it, on the sports staff, and I got the impression Eddie Sawyer thought it was funny to stick Mark Malone with me." Scott nodded, and she figured he knew the newspaper people even better than she did.

"The only thing Mark told me was that I had to write the 'athlete of the week' article and that it was due by one o'clock on Saturday. I'm still not sure if it was just a test or if he really wanted to give me the column. Anyway, I didn't have much choice but to go to the basketball game Friday night and find my athlete of the week there. I'm really sorry if it got you in trouble with the other guys on the team."

She held her breath, afraid he would disappoint her by offering a few comments about incompetent women trying to do things that were out of their league. Learning how badly she'd messed up her first official assignment, she had a few doubts about herself. How could she blame him if he shared them?

"So I guess we both have a few problems," he said with an easy smile.

Sam blinked in surprise. Maybe he was as nice as his hazel eyes suggested. "Thanks for understanding."

"I can relate to your trying to earn a spot on

the newspaper staff. It's not much different from me or any of the other guys fighting for a place on the team."

"Really?" Sam had thought the battle was something personal between her and Mark Malone. She preferred the idea of trying to make the newspaper team.

"Sure. And it's worth all the work. Once you make the team, it'll get better," he promised.

"I hope you're right." Sam hadn't gone to the *Herald* office to be a sportswriter, but it looked like there wasn't much chance of her becoming an investigative reporter. If she was going to make the *Herald* team, it was going to have to be on Mark Malone's squad.

"I don't know if you've ever played any sports, but it's great being part of a team. That's why I had to come see you today. All of us on the basketball team have to work as a group. I couldn't let this article come between us and cause problems."

"Can you take care of it now? I mean, can you give them an explanation they'll be happy with?" She wanted to ask if he was going to tell all the guys that Sam Hill was an idiot. That wouldn't do much for her credibility, but she wouldn't blame him for telling them the truth if it would make the other guys happy. She could see how important team unity was to him.

"I'll just tell them Mark Malone was initiating you. Believe me, he's done worse things to other new reporters—and they were guys!"

Sam's mouth fell open. "Are you kidding me?"

Scott stood, and Sam still couldn't believe how tall he looked, off the court. "No, it's true, but I won't tell you what happened. Some of the guys are still on the staff, and I'll leave it up to them to decide whether or not they want to share their embarrassing stories."

Sam could see Scott was ready to leave, and she felt a little disappointed. He'd been so nice to her that she wanted to spend more time with him, but that was crazy. She was just a reporter doing a story. She'd probably run into him from time to time, but that was it. They weren't friends, just acquaintances.

She pulled herself off the couch and walked him to the door. "Thanks for coming by so we could clear the air." She offered her right hand.

He took it in his and shook it firmly. "I appreciate your honesty. I haven't met a lot of girls around campus like you."

At least he'd noticed she was a girl, Sam consoled herself as his hand opened to let go of hers. She couldn't help noticing how tiny her hand looked in comparison to his. She also couldn't help noticing how nice it felt to hold his hand, if only for a second.

An hour later, Sam was still thinking about him. The sun had gone down and the room was getting dark when Angie came home and snapped on a light.

"Are you moping, or what?" she asked after getting a look at Sam's pensive face.

"I'm beginning to think Roni knows me pretty well," Sam said mysteriously.

"You mean you're giving in to her fluff that your life will be better if you find a guy?" Clearly, Angie thought Sam should have better things to do with her life.

"Not exactly, but I think I've been avoiding men too carefully."

Angie sat cross-legged on her bed. "This sounds interesting."

"Scott O'Connor was here today to talk about the article I wrote. I really liked him," Sam admitted. "But I've given it a lot of thought and decided I've been away from guys too long. Maybe *any* guy could have walked in here today and left me breathless."

"Maybe," Angie said.

Sam wished Angie had agreed with her more wholeheartedly. If it wasn't a matter of her wanting a man's company, then there had to be something special about Scott O'Connor. And knowing how unlikely it was that he was thinking about *her* right now, the last thing Sam needed was a one-sided crush on the Hawthorne Hawks' star center. She'd move straight from sophomore slump to sophomore dump.

Chapter 4

"You mean I'm covering the big game on Friday night? The main article?" Sam was sure she had misunderstood Mark. He couldn't be offering her a chance to write up the men's varsity basketball game.

"What's wrong, Hill?" he challenged. "Don't think you can handle it?"

Sam stuffed her hands in her pants pockets. "Sure. I just wanted to make sure I know what you want."

"What I want is for Chet to do the article, but he has to go home for his sister's wedding," he said bluntly. "And no one else is available."

Although Sam didn't think he had to make it so obvious she was his last choice, she decided it was best to ignore the slight. "Will there be a photographer?" she asked.

Mark laughed. "Considering your questionable talents with the camera, there will be two photographers on the floor. You just have to write."

"Okay."

Mark shoved his glasses back into place on his nose and stared at her. "Got it? Any questions?" he asked impatiently.

"No."

Mark rolled his chair back and crossed his arms over his chest. "Look, Sam. I know I should have told you about Jim Barker breaking that swimming record last week. I heard Scott O'Connor wasn't too pleased with your selection of 'athlete of the week.'"

"No big deal," she said simply. She didn't bother to tell Mark she'd been thinking about Scott ever since he'd come to see her about the article.

"Well, I thought I could give you a few pointers . . . if you think you might need a little help." There was a pained expression on his face, as if offering assistance violated his basic principles of breaking in sports reporters.

"Thanks, Mark. But I'd rather do some research on my own."

He nodded, and Sam knew she'd done the right thing.

Putting her assignment for statistics class out of her mind, Sam settled at a table in the corner of the *Herald* office known as "the archives." She thumbed through old issues of the paper to see how major games and matches were usually covered. The writing was analytical, and only occasionally editorial. Chet, Mark's apparent favorite, liked to talk about "turning points" and "game-winning plays." Sam decided to watch the game with an open mind. She wanted to develop her own style of coverage.

She wasn't sure that was what Mark Malone wanted from her, but then Sam was never sure what her editor had in mind. Had he offered to help her because he actually had a decent side? Or was he giving her a break just because she was a girl? She winced at the thought.

It was Sam's love of writing that had brought her to the paper. Sure, she hadn't been thrilled about doing sports when she first got the assignment, but now it was turning into a challenge. Samantha Hill had something to show Mark and Eddie Sawyer, the editor-in-chief who had thought it was wildly amusing to give Mark a female reporter. If she had to stay up all night, she was going to turn in a first-class article on Friday night's basketball game.

Poking around, she came across a file full of clippings, mostly articles from past *Heralds* organized by subject. When she started looking through the 'basketball' file, Sam found a few stories from other newspapers—some from the Atlanta paper, and others from neighboring colleges the Hawks had competed against. It didn't take Sam long to discover one thing: Scott's name came up often.

A stinging editorial piece written two years ago caught Sam's eye. Apparently, Scott had been the "sixth" man for the Hawks during his sophomore year. The article maintained that Scott was excellent in that position, coming off the bench game after game to revitalize the team. But the writer believed Scott should replace the Hawks' center, a senior who'd been in a slump since the season began. The reporter said Scott agreed, and then went on to hint that Scott was being contacted by some other schools whose coaches would love to have him among their starting five in his junior year.

An Atlanta reporter had seen that article and had come to campus to interview Scott later in the season. Sam smiled as she read Scott's comments about how much he enjoyed being part of the team. Although he said he would like to play more often, he told the man he was willing to play whenever and wherever the coach wanted him, because that was best for the team. The Atlanta reporter concluded that the college sophomore sounded too good to be true, and he left it up to his readers to decide whether or not they thought Scott was entertaining offers from other schools.

Sam didn't have to consider that question for more than two seconds. She'd heard him talk about those same feelings Monday afternoon. Maybe Scott's dedication to the team was a little unusual, but Sam had realized already that he wasn't an average kind of guy. The Scott O'Connor she'd met would have been satisfied as the Hawks' reliable sixth man, willing to help out the team whenever one of the first five men got into trouble.

She wondered what other treasures might be buried in the file. Then she spotted a collection of typewritten sheets: Each page had a team member's name typed at the top, followed by information such as the player's height, weight, and honors. Sam knew she should skim all the sheets, but she had to look at Scott's biography first. Once she set it on the desk to study it, she realized how foolishly she was acting. The guy had only talked to her once, and she couldn't get him out of her mind.

The stat sheet listed his full name as Scott Hampton O'Connor. It had been prepared when he was a freshman, and his hometown was Lexington, Kentucky, where he'd been president of his senior class and a member of the National Honor Society. Scott had won a small scholarship for citizenship, and of course he'd been an outstanding basketball player in high school. After breaking most of his school's records, he was named to the all-state team. To Sam, the stat sheet painted a picture of a nice, well-rounded guy.

In a strange way, Sam was sorry she'd discovered so much about Scott. The more she learned about him, the more she liked him. And it became more and more obvious to her that such a big star wouldn't be interested in an average person like herself. Sam forced herself to take a deep breath and get back to work. She'd opened the files to do research for her article, not to peek into Scott's glorious past.

"Why are you so quiet, tonight, Sam?" Stacy asked as the group devoured a pizza in Suite 3A.

"Has your editor been giving you a bad time again?" Maddie asked, pulling a pizza wedge free from the rest of the pie.

"Not really," Sam said halfheartedly. She'd been feeling down ever since she left the *Herald* office, but it had nothing to do with Mark Malone.

"If I didn't know better, I'd say Sam was heartsick," Roni ventured.

"Give it up, Davies." Stacy dismissed Roni's comment with a wave of her hand. "If you're going to turn this into one more discussion of our nonexistent love lives, then you can just go back to your own room."

Roni held up her hand in protest. "Take a good look at Sam and tell me if I'm wrong. I haven't seen her look so sad since she broke up with Aaron."

Everyone leaned a little closer to look at Sam. Maddie nodded. "I think Roni might actually be right this time."

Sam ducked her head and let her hair fall across her face. She didn't appreciate being inspected by her friends.

"Well, what is it, Sam?" Stacy asked. "*Is* something going on between you and some guy?"

"I wish," Sam finally admitted. "But it's more like a high school crush than anything else." She sighed.

"On Scott O'Connor?" Maddie asked.

"How did you know?" Sam was stunned. She hoped she hadn't been that obvious.

"It was just a lucky guess." Maddie took a bite of her pizza.

"I don't understand why I'm so crazy about him," Sam said with a helpless shrug.

"Don't be silly," Roni said. "He's a hunk."

"No, that's not it."

"You don't think he's the original tall, dark, and handsome man?" Stacy asked. "Because *I* do."

"Of course, I've noticed how good-looking he is," Sam said quickly. "But there's more to him than his hazel eyes, handsome face, and well-proportioned body."

Roni laughed out loud. "I'd say she's noticed!"

"I'm glad to hear it," Stacy declared. "I was getting a little worried there. So, tell us what's so special about Scott."

Sam started to list the things that she liked about him. "He cares about his team. He's understanding. He's modest, too. I was so comfortable talking to him, even though he's such a sports star. He didn't laugh at me for not knowing everything about the sports scene here. Et cetera, et cetera!" Sam finished.

"If he's that great, then why are you sitting

around eating pizza with us?" Stacy wanted to know.

"Well, I felt some magic when I met him, but I'm pretty sure he didn't feel a thing. He probably doesn't even remember what I look like." Sam blushed, knowing she sounded like a high school freshman with a major crush.

"How do you know he hasn't been thinking about you ever since you talked to him Monday afternoon?" Roni inquired.

"He hasn't called me or anything." Not that she'd expected him to, Sam told herself. She hadn't dared hope for anything that wonderful.

"And you haven't called him," Roni said triumphantly.

Sam didn't see why Roni sounded so victorious. "So?"

"He's been on your mind and you haven't made any attempt to contact him. How can you be sure he's not doing the same thing? I think you should call him."

"Me? Call him?" Sam's palms got sweaty at the very thought of dialing his number.

"This is the eighties," Stacy reminded her, getting into the campaign.

"What's the worst that could happen?" Maddie asked.

"I'd say something stupid, he'd find out what a fool I am, and I'd be afraid to ever see him again," Sam said.

"Sometimes you have to take that risk," Stacy advised.

"I understand about risks, but this isn't the right time for me."

"How can you be sure unless you try?" Roni wheedled.

"Look at the history of my love life," Sam requested. "In the past year, I broke up with two guys—and *they* had pursued me! How far do you think I'd get with a guy who isn't even interested?" She shook her head. "This is definitely not the right time for me to make a play for Scott O'Connor."

"See you later, Sam," Stacy called from her doorway.

"Sorry you can't stay," Maddie added. "But you're not the only one that needs to hit the books tonight—so I guess I should say thanks for leaving me to my history reading."

"Sam?"

Just as Sam turned to leave Suite 3A, Jean Jones came out of her room. "Hi, Jean. How's it going?"

"You said we could talk sometime."

"You're right." Sam had almost forgotten that she'd promised to talk to Jean that night she had barely escaped the streakers. "My place or yours?"

"I'd like it to be private," she said shyly.

"Then let's use my room," Sam suggested. "Angie's out somewhere with Tucker."

When they got to Sam's room, Sam pulled out her desk chair and sat down. "What can I do for you?"

"I've got to talk to someone about the basketball team. When I agreed to come to Hawthorne, and they offered me a scholarship, I thought I'd be starting on the varsity team. I've been playing a little in each game, but it's nowhere near what I expected." Jean paced nervously in front of Sam.

"And you think I can help you?" Sam asked.

"I can't exactly talk to the other girls on the team about how much I want their positions," Jean explained. "And you're the only one around here that knows anything about basketball," she pointed out.

Sam appreciated Jean's predicament. Her teammates wouldn't want to hear Jean complain about playing time, and with a roommate like Erica Martin, Jean had no one to turn to with her concerns. Erica would probably tell Jean to quit the team and take up cheerleading.

After asking her friends to help her with her Scott O'Connor obsession, Sam was glad to have the chance to help someone else. "I can't say I have personal experience as an athlete, Jean, but I think I do understand what's happening to you in a general sense. Let me ask you a question: How many kids from your high school class went away to top colleges?"

"I don't know," Jean replied. "Not too many. A quarter?"

"That sounds right. And most of them were the smartest kids. Agreed?" Jean nodded and Sam continued. "That's what happened all around the country. So when all these smart kids get to

Hawthorne, they're competing with other students who are just as smart as they are. They can't all be at the top of the class anymore. "

Jean stopped pacing for a second. She seemed to be thinking about what Sam had said, but it didn't seem that Sam's point had made her feel any better. Sam searched her brain for a sports-related story that might help Jean more. She remembered what she had heard at the *Herald* office about Jim Barker, the swimmer.

"Did you hear about the swimmer who broke a conference record last week?" she asked Jean.

"Yeah, I think so," Jean said slowly.

"I bet you didn't know that he barely made the swim team his freshman year. The coach didn't want him on the team, but he kept working out, and when one of the guys on the team got injured, Jim got his big chance. And he proved to the coach, and everyone else, that he was varsity material."

"So you're saying I have to wait until someone messes up or breaks her ankle before I can be a starter?" Jean asked.

"I suppose you could just wait around. Or you could give up now," Sam told the freshman. "But I think you'd be happier if you kept working as hard as you can. That way, when you *do* get a chance to impress the coach, you'll be ready."

"Yeah?" Jean sounded a little encouraged by Sam's advice.

Sam hoped she'd said the right thing. She wasn't an athlete, but she had learned a few things in her year and a half at Hawthorne, and she knew how important it was for each person to take charge of her own life, and how hard it was to accept that you couldn't always be the best at college because everyone else was so talented. "Jean, I believe it never hurts to do your best."

"Thanks," Jean grinned. "This has helped a lot."

"No problem."

After Jean left, Sam kept thinking about her. Who would have thought anyone would see Sam as some kind of sports expert? If she'd managed to impress Jean, maybe she had a chance to fool Mark with the story she'd write about the men's game Friday night.

Chapter 5

Sam was still thinking about Jean at ten o'clock that night. Something in the back of her mind kept telling her there was one more thing she could do to give Jean some support. The feeling didn't go away while she reviewed her statistics class notes for tomorrow's quiz and leafed through her notes on the reading for her child development class.

"I've got it!" Sam suddenly exclaimed, clapping her hands together in front of her face.

"Got what?" Angie asked, looking up from her desk. "I thought we got rid of all those nasty little gnats when Roni dumped her palm tree in the trash."

Sam laughed. "I didn't kill anything, I just

53

figured something out that's been bothering me all night."

"Whatever it is, it must be good."

"It is." Sam was amazed she hadn't thought of it earlier. The old articles from the *Herald* files on Scott reported that he hadn't exactly taken Hawthorne by storm as a freshman, either. He'd gone from all-state in high school to working his way up to the sixth-man position in his sophomore year. Even Scott O'Connor, a star player, had been frustrated his freshman year. Maybe he could help Jean with her problem.

All Sam had to do was call Scott and ask him to talk with Jean. But her hands shook at the very thought of picking up the phone. Yet, at the same time, she was filled with a happy kind of excitement. It would really help Jean to talk to an older, experienced player.

"You don't look like someone who just solved a problem," Angie observed. "You look like you're trying to talk yourself into doing something you don't want to do."

"It's a little of both," Sam said.

"Tell me all about your dilemma." Angie put down her spiral notebook. "Maybe I can help?"

Sam leaned back in her desk chair. "It goes like this. There's a guy I would like to see again. Tonight everyone said I should call him, but I'm afraid he'll think I'm stupid. Then someone else asked me for help, and I've realized this guy might have the answers to this other person's questions. . . ."

"I get it," Angie announced. "You're afraid that if you have this guy talk to the friend, that he might start liking the friend instead of you. So do you help the friend, or protect your own interests?"

"A good question, but it's not the situation." Sam loved Angie's vivid imagination. "I'm trying to decide if I'd be calling the guy to help the friend, or if I'd be using the friend as an excuse to make the call."

"Another good question." Angie leaned forward and put her chin in her hands, resting her elbows on the desk. "So what are you going to do?"

Sam folded and refolded her hands. "I don't know." She really wanted to call Scott: Just hearing his voice would keep her going for another few days. She hadn't had an all-consuming crush like this since Bob Carr in the eighth grade. Sam had thought she'd outgrown that kind of behavior. But now she was wondering if maybe Scott was the first guy she'd met since Bob Carr who could make her feel so crazy.

"If you want my advice, I think you should call him."

"You do?" Angie was one of the most sensitive persons Sam knew. And if Angie would make the call, then Sam couldn't feel too guilty about it. She picked up the phone and dialed Scott's number. She had already memorized it from the student directory. Gripping the receiver in her left hand, she held her breath until someone answered the phone. She could tell by just the deep "hello" that it was Scott.

"Hi, Scott? This is Samantha Hill." The greeting rushed out of her mouth, and Sam told herself to calm down. She would never be able to ask him a favor if she talked so fast that her tongue got tangled up in the words.

"Sam? The famous girl sports reporter?"

She blushed. "That's me."

"What can I do for you?"

She had a hundred answers to that question, but she decided to stick to the reason for her call. "There's a freshman girl I know who plays basketball. She's not getting as much playing time as she'd like and she's feeling really frustrated. I wondered if you could talk to her."

"You think I'm a frustrated athlete?"

She knew he was teasing, and she guessed there was a sparkle in his hazel eyes. "No, you're a star—don't you know that?"

"If I wasn't one before, you made me one with your article," he told her.

"I thought we were done talking about that," she said, embarrassed he'd brought it up, and embarrassed she'd called him a star. This conversation was not off to a great start, Sam thought.

"We are, don't worry. But what do you think I can do for this girl?"

Sam started to doodle on a scrap of paper. "I tried to tell her that not everyone can be a star their first year. I think it would be more convincing if she heard it from you."

"If you think it would help, I'd be happy to talk with her. What's her name?"

She should have known how easy it would be to ask this incredibly nice guy for the favor. "Her name is Jean Jones. Have you seen her play?"

"Sure. She's the one from Idaho," he said. "I'll look for her tomorrow."

Sam didn't know what to say, now that she'd taken care of the business part of her call. She wanted him to stay on the line longer, but there was nothing more for them to discuss. And if she kept talking, she might end up saying something stupid. "Well . . . thanks, Scott. Sorry to bother you."

"I'm glad to help a fellow athlete," he said cheerfully.

"Good." Sam knew it was time to hang up, but she didn't want to say good-bye.

"Look, I have to get going. I'm working on a paper for my economics class," he told her. "I'll see you around, okay?"

"Sure. I've got to get back to work, too. 'Bye."

She held the receiver to her ear and listened to the click and then the dial tone after Scott was gone.

"Is he going to help Jean?" Angie asked.

"Yeah. He's going to talk with her."

"Then your call was a success," Angie noted.

"Kind of." Sam had hoped for more, even if she didn't know exactly what she had wanted Scott to say.

"I think you've got a bigger problem than

Jean," Angie said sympathetically. "She's playing in some games, and she'll play more as the coach gets to know her. But what are you going to do about this guy?"

"I'm not *that* desperate," Sam said in self defense. At least she hoped things weren't as bad as Angie was making them sound.

"Are you saying he doesn't turn you into jello?"

"Maybe he does, but he doesn't even know I'm alive." Scott had had his chance to make friendly small talk, and he'd stuck to business instead, hurrying to get back to his economics assignment. "I have to forget him."

"It seems like a shame to give up," Angie said.

"Yeah, but I have to be realistic," Sam said bravely. "Besides, I'm too busy to mope around over some guy who doesn't want me."

Sam heard a jingling sound outside her door Thursday afternoon. It sounded as if Santa Claus and his reindeer had landed in the living room. Then she heard a muffled "Help!" come from the other side of the door. Sam hurried to let whoever it was inside.

"Is that you, Angie?" Sam asked when all she saw was a large box with arms wrapped around it.

Angie peeked around the side of the box. "Of course it is."

Sam helped Angie set the box on the floor between the beds. Angie plunged her hands into the box and pulled out two buttons. She handed one to Sam. "Aren't these great?"

Sam turned the button over and read the message on the front: SAVE THE MONKEYS. "Where did you get these?" she asked Angie.

"At this printing store downtown. They were Tucker's idea to promote the campaign for those poor animals being shipped to the psychology department." Angie held her button in the palm of her hand, turning it at various angles so that Sam would fully appreciate its appeal. "Will you wear one?"

"What do they cost?"

"Nothing. I'm giving them away," Angie said.

"Didn't it cost a lot of money to have them made?" Sam didn't want to underestimate Angie, but it was hard to believe her roommate could have gotten someone to donate all those buttons.

"Tucker knew someone who gave me a deal."

Sam should have expected that answer. "But how are you paying for these if you're not going to sell them?"

"I bought them with some of the money I made selling jewelry." Angie looked at the box. "How do you think I should distribute them? Tucker and I thought one way to get the campaign started would be to hand buttons out to people we know. That way they'll help spread the message."

Sam shook her head in amazement. Angie was so dedicated that it was inspiring. "I'll be happy to wear a button around, and I'll carry a couple in my knapsack to hand out if anyone asks about it."

"Thanks!" Angie tossed her hair over her shoulders and flashed a smile at Sam.

"But is there more to your campaign?" Sam asked. "The buttons are great, but what will they do?"

"They'll let people know about the campaign, so they'll want to come to the demonstration at the psych building two weeks from Saturday."

Sam sat on the edge of her bed. "Why don't you tell me about it? In case someone asks me when I'm wearing my button."

Angie sat down on her bed and hugged her knees to her chest. "You're great, Sam. I just want to have students gather around the building to show the faculty how we feel about their plans for research."

"Are you planning to have people carry signs? Will someone be making a speech with a microphone?" Sam asked.

"There will be speakers," Angie told her. "But I hadn't thought about signs. Do you think they're a good idea?"

Sam laughed. "Don't ask me. I just wanted to warn you to check out the student handbook. I really got burned my freshman year when I got drawn into an illegal demonstration."

"You?" Angie's mouth fell open in disbelief.

"Yes, me." Sam lifted her chin proudly. "I almost got suspended."

"You're making this up."

"I am not," Sam said indignantly. "It was in my political science class, first semester. We were supposed to do some kind of activity project and I was in a group with a guy who wanted to get a lot of attention. While the rest of us thought we were picketing the trustee meeting because the school still held some stock in companies in South Africa, our leader purposely got us arrested by the Hawthorne security guards—"

"*You* got busted?" Angie interrupted. "What for?"

"We broke school rules: demonstrating without a permit, unauthorized assembly, and the unapproved use of a PA system. I think there was something wrong with *where* we met, too. Some of the other students were charged with resisting arrest."

"Did you wimp out on them, Sam?" There was a laughing glimmer in Angie's blue eyes.

"I wouldn't call it 'wimping out,'" Sam said. "The protest had been misrepresented to me, and I didn't feel any obligation to see it through to the very end. Not that I don't believe in keeping out of South Africa until they make some changes in that country, but getting suspended wasn't part of the deal that afternoon."

"Sounds like you did the right thing," Angie said, surprising Sam. "You have to feel strongly about something before it's right to take those kinds of risks."

"You've done it before."

"Lots of times. I'm willing to put a lot of effort into the monkey deal, but there's no reason to take unnecessary risks. I'll check out the handbook and get all the required permits."

"Smart girl," Sam observed aloud.

"With a little help from my friends." Angie blushed slightly at her sentimental comment. "What I mean is, I appreciate your advice."

"No problem. Now where is my button?"

Angie pointed to the spot where Sam had set it on her bedspread. They both laughed when she pinned it to her Hawthorne College sweatshirt.

"Who knows?" Sam raised her eyebrows. "We could be starting a new fashion trend."

A knock on the door surprised them both.

"Expecting anyone?" Angie asked.

"No, unless it's the fashion reporter from the *Herald* coming to take some pictures of us wearing these hot new buttons," Sam teased on her way to the door. She practically fainted when she saw who was waiting for her.

"Hi, Sam," Scott said from the hallway. When she didn't move back or step aside, he asked, "May I come in for a few minutes?"

Sam nearly tripped over her feet, just like the last time Scott had visited, as she backed up toward her room. "Sure. Be my guest."

Angie only needed one look at Sam's nervous face and the gorgeous guy coming into the room, and she apparently knew he was the object of her roommate's uncontrollable crush. She smiled at Sam. "I'm going to take these around to some friends. I'll catch up with you later, okay?"

"What?" Sam squinted at the button box as if

she'd never seen it before. "Oh, yeah. Right. I'll see you later."

"I didn't mean to scare your friend away," Scott said after Angie had disappeared.

Sam couldn't decide whether to sit down or stand across the room from him. He was so tall that she felt like a midget when she sat down, but her knees were too weak to stand.

"Am I making you nervous or something?" he asked.

Sam just stared at Scott. He looked so at ease with his hands in the pockets of his green Hawthorne letter jacket. His long legs were covered by worn blue jeans. How could he seem so cool when her head was spinning and her tongue was stuck to the roof of her mouth?

"Sam, did you hear me? Are you expecting someone else? Am I in the way?" Scott asked.

"No," she finally managed to squeak. "Not at all. Sorry if I seem out of it," Sam apologized.

"That's okay. I hoped we could talk a little bit. Maybe we could go for a walk," he suggested.

"I'd like that." The room seemed incredibly small with the two of them in it together, and Sam hoped the fresh air outside would clear her head so Scott wouldn't think she was a complete idiot.

He opened the door and waited for Sam to step into the hall. Closing it behind him, he said, "Let's walk down by the lake."

She nodded and tried to settle the butterflies in her stomach by taking a few deep breaths, as quietly as she could. She concentrated on breathing in for two counts and breathing out for two counts while she walked alongside Scott.

"Am I walking too fast for you?" he asked, looking down at her.

"No. I'm fine."

"But you're breathing so hard. Don't be shy," he told her. "You can tell me I'm walking too fast. Sometimes I forget how long my legs are."

Sam couldn't help it—she had to laugh. It felt good, as if she'd released a lot of her tension just by giggling.

"I like the way you laugh," Scott said, to Sam's utter amazement.

"Uh, thanks." She wanted to ask him why he liked it and how it sounded to him, but she didn't want to analyze the compliment to death. She was thrilled to hear he liked *anything* about her, especially since she was having such a hard time just talking to him.

"We're here," he announced as they reached the edge of Hawthorne Lake. Scott found an empty bench and sat down, patting the spot next to him. "Would you like to have a seat?"

You bet, Sam screamed inside.

Chapter 6

Scott leaned back against the bench and rested his hands on his thighs. "I talked to Jean this morning."

"You did? How did it go?"

He nodded his head. "I think it went really well."

"What did you say? What did *she* say?" Sam asked.

He smiled. "Look, I asked you out here to talk about you, not Jean Jones."

"Me?" Sam wondered if she was dreaming.

"Your call surprised me," he told her. "Don't take this wrong, but the first time I met you I didn't think you were the kind of person who would be so concerned about another girl's future in basketball."

"What *did* you think I'd care about?" she asked, honestly curious about the impression she'd made on him. She certainly remembered how she'd felt about him after their first meeting.

"Now you're trying to embarrass me." He sighed. "I guess I thought you were like a lot of the other girls around here . . . concerned about your clothes, and your hair, and your plans for Friday night."

"That sounds awfully shallow. None of my girlfriends are like that," she argued.

"Okay, I'm sorry. But some of the girls I've met here are like that. You were a little more interesting because you're a reporter," he admitted.

"Actually, I'm going to be a teacher if I ever graduate from this place." Though graduating from Hawthorne right now was the last thing she wanted to do, Sam thought.

"So why are you writing the sports column?" he asked, turning his head to get a better look at her.

"I needed something else to do this semester," she said vaguely.

"You have enough extra time to be bored?"

"I wasn't bored, I just wanted to get involved in something new, and interesting." Sam had been looking for some excitement. School simply hadn't been as much fun for her this year. Maybe it was losing Aaron, or maybe it was sophomore slump; but Sam would keep those considerations to herself.

"Okay," he said, cheerfully letting his questions

drop. "I hope you're planning to teach little kids."

"I'm working toward elementary certification."

"Good." He stretched his right foot out in front of the bench and stared at it. "I think it might be hard for high school boys to concentrate with you behind the desk."

"Excuse me?" Sam knew she'd heard him correctly, but she couldn't believe he was paying her another compliment. She leaned forward to get a glimpse of his face, and she was stunned to see a broad grin. "What's so funny?"

"You are, Samantha."

"Thanks a lot," she mumbled.

"Don't misunderstand me," he appealed. "But the guys said you were probably only calling about Jean because you wanted to get in good with me. They also thought you'd be the kind of girl who would appreciate flattering comments. I can see now how wrong they were—you're nothing like that."

"That's great," she said cynically. The more she heard about "the guys" the less she liked them. First, they thought she'd written the column on Scott because she liked him. And now they thought she'd been using Jean's problems to her own advantage.

His right hand reached out toward her, but then he pulled it back and rested it on his leg. "I didn't *want* to believe them. I'm glad you proved the guys wrong," he said shyly.

When he put it that way, Sam had to stop being so critical. He was trying to tell her she'd passed some kind of test; but her forgiveness of Scott didn't extend to his buddies. "Your friends seem to have a very low opinion of Hawthorne women."

"Don't be too hard on them," he requested. "All the guys on the team look out for each other. You wouldn't believe what a few girls have done to get our attention."

"I suppose you do have a lot of fans," she said, starting to understand.

"It's not the fans we have problems with," he muttered. "It's the groupies. Unfortunately, they can make a guy pretty suspicious."

It struck Sam that some guys wouldn't mind having girls chasing them around and offering favors. But Scott obviously did. Once again, her opinion of him rose even higher. He wanted friends who liked him for himself, not for his popularity. She was seeing more sides to Scott O'Connor than just the basketball star image, and she was glad.

"Well," Sam continued, trying to get back to the original topic of conversation, "if it's true you're convinced I really care about Jean, could you tell me how things went with her?"

Scott nodded. "We talked for a long time about how I'd felt as a freshman, when I wasn't getting as much playing time as I thought I deserved. We discussed how similar her experiences, so far, are to mine. After that, I told her how important it is to be part of the team. She agreed to try thinking more of the team, and to do her best for it whenever she has a chance."

Sam turned sideways on the bench to face Scott. "That's super. I hope your advice will make it a little easier for her to adjust to college sports. The competition's a little tougher than in high school."

"That's for sure," he said wholeheartedly. "I guess you got me to help Jean because you'd heard how rough my first two years were here. But how do you know that? Aren't you just a sophomore?"

Sam wondered how he knew she was a sophomore; maybe he'd been doing some research on her, too. "I was looking through some old articles in the *Herald* files the other day."

"Checking me out?" he inquired with a good-natured chuckle.

"No." Sam was glad she had a good excuse for doing the reading. "I was doing research because I'm covering the game Friday night."

"What happened to Chet?" Scott asked.

"He's going home for his sister's wedding." Sam was curious: Would all "the guys" be expecting Chet to write the article? Would anyone even read it when they saw she'd written it?

"Well, if you've read the old articles then you know I thought I was pretty hot stuff as a freshman and sophomore. Even though plenty of guys would love being the sixth man on the team, I was disappointed I wasn't one of the starting five," Scott explained.

"What made you change your attitude?"

"A senior who didn't see much playing time, but loved being part of the team." Scott smiled at the memory of his friend. "He told me how special it was just to be part of the team. He made a contribution by working hard, and keeping up the team's morale. He really opened my eyes, made me see there were other things that were more important than my field goal percentage."

"I'm glad you could do the same thing for Jean." Sam felt she had done the right thing by calling Scott. She could tell he had been pleased to pass along some good advice.

"I just hope I did it half as well," he said humbly.

Sam wanted to share her feelings with him but she didn't want to go overboard. She swallowed hard. "I'm sure you did. I really admire your team philosophy," she told him.

"Thanks. It's not always easy to stick with it. Like when I twisted my ankle during a game last year. I was furious at Coach Tupper when he made me sit out the rest of the game. Sure, I understood he was doing it because the team needed me healthy for our next game, and because he was worried I might hurt it worse if I kept playing that night when the team could win without me, but that didn't help. I still wanted to play."

"It just proves you're human," Sam said. She still couldn't believe how dedicated he was.

He cleared his throat. "Yeah, I guess so. I don't want to talk about me any longer. Can I ask you something, Sam? It's kind of personal."

"Sure."

"I couldn't help noticing your pin." He pointed to her Save the Monkeys button. "What does it mean?"

"My roommate is waging a campaign against the psych department's plan to experiment on chimpanzees," she explained. "The buttons are supposed to encourage conversation and promote the demonstration she's planning."

"Is your roommate that redheaded girl with the love beads who was in your room just now?" he asked.

Sam smiled. People described Angie in very unique ways. "Her name is Angie Perelli."

"I've heard she's kind of strange," he ventured. "What do you think of her?"

"She's a good friend to have," Sam said. "I guess some people think her projects are unusual—setting up recycling barrels, cleaning up the nature trail—but I really respect the way she stands up for the causes she believes in."

"I suppose you'd have to get into that kind of thing, being Aaron Goldberg's girlfriend."

Sam felt her mouth fall open, and she forced it shut. Had Scott O'Connor noticed her long before she wrote the column about him? But then, everyone on campus knew Aaron Goldberg. Even if Scott hadn't seen her with him last year, plenty of other people had.

"I used to be Aaron's girlfriend," she said.

"But you're not anymore?"

"We broke up last summer," Sam answered. She hoped he wouldn't ask why. After explaining it to all her friends, she wanted the painful memories to be part of her past.

"In that case, what are you doing Saturday?" Scott said.

Sam had to bite her lip to keep from squealing. It seemed that he was going to ask her out, but she tried to stay calm. After all, he could have a lot of things in mind besides a date. "Not much—I have to hand in my article on the game by one o'clock, though."

"Do you think you could finish it by ten?"

"If I stay up late Friday night," she said slowly. "Is there some reason I should?"

Scott ran his left hand through his hair. "Some of the guys are going to a basketball clinic in Atlanta and I thought you might like to come along. You know, do some more research?"

"It sounds interesting, but someone else on the staff is probably covering that story."

"No, you misunderstood me," he said. "We're going to Atlanta to teach basketball to children. I want you to go as my guest, not as a reporter."

"Oh." After telling herself to stop hoping for a miracle, Sam was afraid to believe her own ears.

He rubbed his hands together. "Maybe watching a bunch of kids dribble balls around a gym doesn't sound like much fun to you, but we could do something in town afterwards."

"No, it sounds great!" she said quickly. The last thing she wanted was for Scott to change his mind because he thought she wasn't interested. "I'll be ready by ten. I promise."

Sam adjusted her jacket beneath her, trying to get a little more comfortable on the bleachers. From the look of things, the Hawthorne players would be spending most of the afternoon working with the young boys on the gym floor below her. When the woman in front of her turned around, Sam wondered if she had accidentally kicked her. Sam leaned forward. "I'm sorry if I bumped you."

"You didn't," the woman replied. "I just wanted to ask if you'd come down from Hawthorne with the boys."

"Yes."

"Are you involved with the team?" she asked.

Sam wasn't even sure she was involved with one of the team players. "No, actually one of the guys just invited me down for the day."

The woman gathered her coat and purse and moved up one level to sit next to Sam. "Could I ask which one?"

Sam pointed toward the right end of the gym. "The one with the green shorts and yellow high tops . . . the Hawthorne school colors."

"Oh, Scott," the woman said with an approving smile.

"You know him?" Sam asked, incredulous.

"Let me introduce myself," the woman offered.

"My name is Sheila Patterson, and I work for the Atlanta social services department. Each month we have a different activity for fatherless boys. Scott's been working with us since last year. Besides teaching basketball skills, he's helped chaperon all kinds of activities."

"He's a pretty amazing guy." Sam wondered how much longer she would learn something new about Scott every time she turned around. It seemed as if Scott's dedication to helping others extended far beyond the basketball squad.

"He's been a big help to us," the woman said. "The boys think he's great, and several of them have older sisters who wouldn't mind meeting a guy just like him—though I doubt there *are* any more."

Sam laughed, knowing how easy it was to come under Scott O'Connor's spell. She turned her attention back to the basketball court and watched as the boys tried to imitate the moves the older guys were teaching them. Balls kept bouncing away as they attempted to dribble them the length of the gym. The passing drills went a little better, but Sam had to bite her lower lip to keep from laughing when the Hawthorne players gave the boys free time to take shots.

When the Hawthorne team played, the guys made the moves look so simple. They dribbled down the court and around their competitors as if it were the most natural thing in the world to do. Balls shot from impossible positions went through the hoop more often than they missed.

Watching the little boys struggle with basic drills, Sam appreciated how many years the college men had worked to play the way they did. She especially realized how hard Scott had worked to develop his smooth, deadly style.

The team members broke the boys up into four teams for scrimmages. There were tears in Sam's eyes from laughing too hard by the time the first short game reached halftime. The boys had tried to remember all the rules for five minutes, and then the game had turned to chaos, as they ran down the court with the ball hugged against their chests, and then pushed each other under the basket. Scott had whistled foul the first ten violations, but then he gave up. He looked up at Sam and shrugged. She knew what he was saying: The boys were having too much fun for him to spoil it.

After the clinic was over, Sam sat on the bottom bleacher step to wait for Scott. Spending the afternoon at the clinic had been a nice break from her study routine, she decided. More important, she'd learned even more about Scott. Aaron Goldberg wasn't the only Hawthorne student who was trying to make a difference in people's lives.

The gym door opened, and Scott strode across the floor toward the bleachers. "Where are the other guys?" she asked.

"They're heading back to campus. Most of them have dates tonight." He reached for Sam's hands and pulled her to her feet. "Tired of sitting around?"

"Not really," she told him, liking the way his still-damp hair stuck to his forehead. "I had a good time. I think it's great the way you help these boys."

"Really?"

"Yeah." She hurried to keep up with his longer stride as they left the gym. "At first they just looked like a bunch of kids, but the more I watched them, the more I noticed how excited they were about learning from you. They have hopes and dreams like all of us and with people like you helping them, maybe they'll get where they want to."

"You know what I think?" He ruffled the hair at the top of her head and didn't wait for her to reply. "I think you spent too much time with Aaron Goldberg before you guys broke up."

"What do you mean by that? You don't help the boys as a community service?" she asked.

"I guess you could call it community service, but I'm not a worldwide do-gooder like Aaron. I only do this because it makes me feel good."

Sam smiled. She liked that explanation. With Aaron, she'd always felt a little strange that she didn't share his intense dedication to serving others. But she could relate to doing something for someone else just because it felt right to do it.

"Are you disappointed?" he asked as they reached his car in the parking lot. "I mean, did you want to spend the evening discussing the effect of single-parent families on today's society?"

As he opened the passenger door of his red Porsche and helped her slip inside, Sam knew she'd been wrong to think Scott was anything like her ex-boyfriend. Aaron wouldn't be caught dead driving a Porsche; he would have used the money to set up a soup kitchen for the hungry.

Scott peered across the car to stare at Sam, now sitting comfortably in the soft leather passenger seat. "Hey, you really are lost in thought. Have I disappointed you? Would you like to talk some more about the clinic?"

She looked at the concern in his eyes and smiled. "I like your attitude—doing what feels right without analyzing it to death. What did you have planned for tonight?"

"Just that," he told her with a wicked grin. "Fun without analysis."

Sam swallowed twice and tried not to let her imagination run wild. She'd felt safe with Scott so far, and she decided to trust him. "Sounds good to me. Let's get going."

Chapter 7

"The circus?" Sam said under her breath for the third time since they had walked into the auditorium. She had expected Scott to pull his Porsche up to some trendy club in Atlanta where they could dance away the next few hours. Instead, they were sitting behind a giggling troop of Brownies.

"How about some cotton candy?" he asked, spotting a vendor coming up the aisle.

In her wildest dreams, Sam couldn't imagine eating a pink fluff ball with Scott at her side. She loved cotton candy, but she always managed to get some of it stuck to her face and hair. "I don't think so," she told him.

"But you have to," he insisted. Scott pulled some bills from his back pocket and held up two fingers for the vendor. "We can't go to the circus and not eat," he admonished. "That would be un-American."

Sam passed the money down the row towards the vendor, and two pink cotton candies came back on the same route. Sam was still trying to figure out how to eat it without making a mess when the performers started to parade around the arena.

"I haven't been to a circus since the fifth grade," she whispered to him.

"That's a crime," he said, not taking his eyes off the parade. "When I got too old to go by myself, I used to take my little cousins whenever the circus came to Lexington."

Sam buried her face in her cotton candy. The same guy who worked hard to lead the Hawthorne Hawks to victory, and spent his free time with fatherless boys, loved the circus. How had she been lucky enough to fall for him before she even knew what a great guy he was?

Scott's large hand suddenly loomed in her face. She looked up in surprise as he peeled a candied strand of hair off her face. "You're supposed to eat this stuff, not wear it."

She noticed a wisp of candy on his cheek and reached out to touch him. "The same goes for you," she said, trying to keep her voice steady.

Her finger tingled the second it made contact with his cheek. Once she'd wiped off the candy, she knew she should take her hand back, but her finger seemed to be stuck to his skin. Sam forced a smile to cover her embarrassment. She hadn't felt this silly since her very first date.

When he grinned back at her, her finger felt like a part of her hand again and she was able to pull it away. Hoping to control her nerves, she wrapped the rest of her candy in the plastic bag it had come in, and folded her hands in her lap.

"It's the elephants!" Scott cried, seemingly unaware of Sam's inner struggle to keep cool.

Together they watched an elephant wrap his trunk around a girl in a glittering leotard. They held their breaths over the daring flips the trapeze artists executed overhead. And they giggled over the twenty clowns who squeezed into a little car. When Sam's stomach started to hurt from laughing so hard and she tried to put her right hand over her abdomen, she realized Scott was holding it tightly. She stared at their joined hands between the seats and wondered when he had taken her hand. Or had she unconsciously reached for him?

He let go of her hand and gripped her elbow as the last clown waved good-bye to the crowd. "Are you hungry for some real food?"

"You bet I am." They had skipped lunch, and she'd come down from the sugar high the cotton candy had provided.

"How do you feel about hamburgers?" he asked.

"They taste great with a cherry Coke." Sam followed Scott as he found his way through the crowd. She didn't need to worry about losing sight of him; he towered over everyone.

Scott drove to a diner off the highway on their way out of town. After they chose a booth in the corner, they slid onto opposite cushions.

"Oops—excuse me," she said when her foot bumped his tennis shoe.

"It's not your fault." Scott shrugged. "There's never enough room for my legs under restaurant tables. If you'll move a little to one side, I'll angle my legs in the other direction."

After they placed their orders, Sam rested her forearms on the table. "I've had a lot of fun today. Life can get pretty crazy with newspaper deadlines, history reading, and statistics assignments. Thanks for taking me away from it all."

He shifted in his seat and tugged on the bottom of his sweatshirt. "You're not like most of the girls I've met at Hawthorne."

"Is that good or bad?"

"Oh, it's good," he said quickly. "I've had a great time today, too. Thanks for being such a good sport."

"It was my pleasure, sir." Sam batted her eyelashes, doing her best impression of a southern belle.

"I'm serious," he told her. "but I can see how this wouldn't be a very exciting day for someone who used to hang around with Aaron Goldberg."

"Do you want to talk about Aaron?" she asked him cautiously.

"Only if you do." He rearranged the salt and pepper shakers.

"Things were usually pretty serious around Aaron. I mean, when a guy's worried about human dignity and homes for the homeless, life is pretty dramatic." Privately, Sam acknowledged they had shared some wonderful personal times, but Aaron's concern for everyone's welfare had often left her awed and exhausted.

"Today must have been pretty dull by comparison, maybe even frivolous," he said.

"I had fun," she said again, hoping he would believe her. "Sometimes with Aaron I felt like a spectator while I watched him saving the world. Today, I felt like a part of things. Even at the clinic, Sheila described the program to me and I enjoyed watching the boys after I knew a few things about them."

"But was it worth staying up late to finish your article last night?" he inquired, sounding and looking much more at ease.

"You wouldn't be asking what I had to say about last night's game, would you?" she countered.

"I wouldn't dream of prying that information out of you," he deadpanned. "Don't you have journalistic ethics or something?"

She bit her lip and tried to remember if Mark or Eddie had mentioned anything like that. "I'm new on the staff. I'll have to check into it."

"You know, I don't remember any other guys on the team dating a sports reporter . . . but then you're the first girl on the sports staff since I've been at Hawthorne. I hope it's not a conflict of interest or anything."

"Are you serious?" She hadn't thought at all about her interest in Scott being a problem.

"Not too serious," he said as the waitress set baskets of food in front of each of them. He poured some ketchup on his french fries and continued, "I'd just be sorry to have the paper come between us. I'd like to see you again, Sam, but I wouldn't ask you to give up your job for me."

"It's not exactly a job," she replied, correcting him. Sam didn't want to even try to tell him how much she'd like to see him again—she would probably end up tongue-tied. "I mean, they don't pay me or anything."

"Still, I can tell you like working on the *Herald*." He pulled the pickle out of his hamburger.

"You're right. I do like it." His concern for her activities made Sam feel warm inside. She didn't remember any guy she'd dated taking her interests into consideration as Scott just had. Jon had tried to mold her plans to match his. Aaron had left her to follow her own goals, but in all honesty, he hadn't offered her tons of support. It was no wonder she'd liked Scott from the beginning.

"I was just thinking it never hurts to have friends in important places." He couldn't keep a straight face, and Sam laughed when he broke into a grin. "I bet you're expecting me to ask what you wrote in the article. Don't worry. I won't. But did I come out sounding good?"

"Good? If you thought I praised you in the athlete-of-the-week column, just wait until you read my analysis of Friday's game!" she joked.

He covered his face with his hands, leaving a crack between two fingers on his right hand so he could peek through it. His voice was muffled when he confessed, "The thought of it makes my knees shake. You'd better be kidding, Hill."

She decided to let Scott worry about it. After all, her knees had been shaking ever since he had charged into her room on Monday. It was only fair that she let him suffer the same fate for a while.

"I usually eat with some of the guys, but we could sit by the windows today," Scott told Sam as they stood with their Sunday brunches balancing on their trays at the end of the cafeteria line.

Sam noticed the sun streaming through the windows and spied just two empty tables at that end of the dining room. "I'd like to sit over there, but we'd better hurry."

Just like after the circus, Scott strode around the tables and wove through the knots of people having conversations in the aisles. Sam had no problem keeping him in sight, but it wasn't that easy to balance her dishes on her tray as she scurried to catch up with him.

Her soup bowl was ready to slide off the tray by the time they reached a small table next to the windows overlooking the lake. More concerned with Scott and the glances coming in their direction, Sam didn't notice her chicken noodle soup inching toward the edge of her tray. Scott rescued her bowl just as it was about to slide off and spill noodles and broth all over him.

"Hey, look out!" he cried, grabbing a napkin to wipe a few drops of hot liquid off his hands.

"Sorry. I couldn't help noticing all the people watching you," she said as an excuse.

"Who says they're watching me? Maybe all the eyes are on *you*," he suggested, pulling out her chair.

Only Roni, Stacy, and Maddie were watching her, she was tempted to say. Instead she told him, "Most likely they were just trying to see who was running to keep up with you as you raced across the room."

"Making fun of me again, are you?" His eyes were dancing as he sat down and tried to settle into his seat.

Sam remembered the routine from yesterday. "I'm moving my legs to the right, so you should have plenty of room on the window side of the table."

"You catch on quickly, kid," he teased, stealing the cherry off the top of her cottage cheese plate.

"Do you want the whole salad?" she asked.

"I'd rather eat a wet dishrag than cottage cheese." He wrinkled his nose to make his point. "But my coach says I need to eat more fruit."

"Why are you in such a good mood today?" she asked.

"Why shouldn't I be? I'm having lunch with a girl who enjoys the circus. I was beginning to think I was the only person over ten who still thought it was funny to watch clowns tumble out of a tiny car."

Sam wouldn't swear in a courtroom that he was complimenting her, but it sure sounded a lot like flattery. Suddenly she was more interested in leaning on the table and staring at Scott than in eating. "I have to admit you're a surprise to me, too. I didn't expect the school's star basketball player to be a cotton candy fanatic."

"Shhh . . ." Scott's hazel eyes opened wide and he pressed a finger against his lips. "Don't say that too loudly. Coach Tupper hates when we eat candy!"

Scott wanted to spend the afternoon with Sam, but she had to get back to Rogers House to tackle the books she'd neglected all weekend. Scott insisted on walking her back to her dorm, and Sam was happy to accept. After strolling over the bridge across the lake, Sam paused on the second step in front of the dorm while Scott stood below.

"Thanks for lunch," she said, leaning against the stone railing.

"Don't thank me. It's not like I cooked it or anything."

"But the mystery meat tasted better than usual today." Sam tucked her hair behind her ears and smiled. "It must have been the company."

Scott didn't smile back. "I noticed the same thing," he said in a serious tone.

Sam found herself staring into his eyes: They spoke of feelings that he wouldn't or couldn't put into words. She wanted to forget the three chapters she was supposed to read for child psychology and gaze into those bright hazel eyes all afternoon. But she had to be practical. "I've got to get to work."

"It wouldn't hurt if I hit the books for a while, too," he said with a sigh.

"You mean star athletes have to study?"

He leaned close as if prepared to share a secret with her. "Haven't you ever heard of the NCAA rules? We have to get passing grades or else we're off the team."

"And Coach Tupper enforces that rule?" Although she figured Scott would keep his grades up as a matter of principle, she assumed not all the guys would.

"I've seen the coach sit in a guy's room to make sure he studied for a big test," he told her.

Sam put her hands in her jacket pockets to warm them. "I'd hate to get you into any trouble with the coach," she said.

"I'll leave now, but only if you'll promise we can see each other again." He took two steps back and waited for her answer.

"I can guarantee it," she said boldly.

Sam stood on the steps and watched Scott walk away until he was out of sight. Then, determined to tackle her studying, she headed up the stairs. But as she passed by Suite 3A, someone grabbed her and dragged her into the living room.

"Okay, we want to hear *everything*," Stacy demanded.

"Really," Roni added. "Last night all you told us was that you'd had a *good* time. It must have been better than that if Scott O'Connor paraded you in front of the entire school at Sunday brunch."

"He didn't do that," Sam protested.

"What do you call it?" Maddie asked as she shut the door, trapping Sam in the room with her inquisitors.

"We wanted to sit by the windows, and they just happen to be on the opposite side of the dining room from the cafeteria line," she told them stubbornly. She hadn't been flaunting Scott any more than he'd been flaunting her.

"But how did you get the boy to eat brunch with you in front of the whole world?" Roni wanted to know.

"He just called this morning and said he'd like to see me, since we had such a good time together yesterday," Sam explained.

"And that's another matter." Stacy stood and came face to face with Sam. "What really happened yesterday that made him so interested in you?"

"We went to the circus. I ate cotton candy and laughed at the clowns with him." Sam stared back at Stacy.

"And that was all it took to get the most eligible hunk on campus eating out of your hand?" Stacy demanded.

"He's not actually eating out of my hand, but he did steal part of my brunch." Sam couldn't help teasing her friends.

"Come on, Sam. Get serious," Roni demanded, wringing her hands. "What's going on between you and Scott O'Connor?"

"Roni, have you ever considered a career as a reporter?" Sam joked. "Serious. Okay. I think we've got to know each other a little bit before there gets to be a boy-girl thing between us. I wanted to give him time to find out I'm not like the girls who chase him all over campus. He's spending some time with me because we have fun together," she concluded.

"It all sounds too simple," Roni moaned.

"I think it's a matter of being in the right place at the right time," Stacy decided.

"Is he as wonderful as you thought he would be?" Maddie asked wistfully.

"He's even better," Sam answered enthusiastically. "He's loyal to his friends, he cares about others, he's funny—"

"Don't forget he's gorgeous," Stacy reminded her.

Sam fanned her face with her hand. "Don't worry, I won't."

The door to one of the bedrooms opened and Erica poked her head into the room. "Are you guys talking about Scott O'Connor?"

"We were asking Sam what it's like to go out with him," Roni said, trying to make it plain to Erica that she should keep her hands off of him.

"I saw you with him at lunch," Erica said to Sam. "Is he taken?"

Sam grinned at Erica's blunt question. "Taken? Not exactly. But I would say he's a little busy right now."

"Oh, really? Hm." Erica went back into her room and closed the door.

"Why didn't you tell her to leave him alone?" Maddie whispered to Sam.

Sam shook her head. "She's just the kind of girl that Scott seems to avoid like the plague. I'm not worried. Plus, the last thing I need is a campus-wide rumor that O'Connor and Hill are the newest couple on campus."

"You're playing it pretty cool for a girl who said just a few days ago that she wasn't any good at catching a guy," Roni observed.

"No one's doing any catching," Sam insisted, trying to make them understand how naturally things were happening between her and Scott. "We just like each other."

Chapter 8

"Glad you could make it, Hill." Mark was sitting on the edge of his desk with the other three sports reporters standing around him.

"Just got your message," she said, refusing to let him embarrass her in front of the guys. Angie had taped a note to their door, but Sam hadn't gone back to her room until after her two o'clock class.

Sam pushed aside some papers on the far end of Mark's desk and leaned against it. "Did y'all read my editorial in today's paper?" Mark asked.

Sam had read it with great interest. She had been impressed by Mark's persuasive style. He was concerned with the rumors circulating around campus that involved NCAA violations by Hawthorne athletes, coaches, and faculty members. He'd said it was easy to jump to conclusions or to make up stories about the athletes, but the time had come for someone to get to the bottom of the whispered accusations. The editorial had ended with the announcement that next week the *Herald* would be kicking off a series of investigative articles addressing those very questions.

"It's about time we got involved with NCAA violations," Chet said. "With all the rumors floating around campus, we can do a real service to the community by getting the stories straight."

"Right! I can't wait to get some dirt on some of these athletes," the guy who had followed the football team last fall commented.

Mark held up his hand. "Wait a minute! I don't have any hatchet jobs in mind. I imagine we'll find a few people who've bent some of the rules, but I'm betting most of the serious rumors will be unfounded."

"It is up to us to find the truth," Sam added. She had come to the *Herald* office hoping to do some investigative reporting, but she never thought she'd end up doing her digging for the sports page.

Mark stared at Sam. "Think you can handle the heavy responsibility?" he asked her in a patronizing tone.

The other guys snickered and Sam examined her fingernails, pretending not to be bothered in the least. "Do we each pick which stories we want to track, or do you have assignments for us?" she inquired, ignoring his rude query.

"Are you in a hurry or something?" Mark asked. "Don't you like hanging out with us?"

"You guys are great," she said, rolling her eyes. "But I've got a discussion section for my statistics class in half an hour, and I don't want to be late."

"Hand out the assignments," Chet urged Mark. "Sam needs help with her statistics, in case you hadn't noticed."

Sam frowned at Chet.

"All right, hold on a second," Mark said, rustling through a file. Then he handed each of them a typed sheet with a list of names and allegations.

There were three entries on Sam's sheet. The first concerned Tom Moore, a junior on the basketball team. He'd flown home almost every other weekend first semester, and no one knew where he was getting the money. Her second assignment was Deb Wilson, a starter on the girls' basketball team who had supposedly failed American literature. Sam glanced at the third entry. She blinked and looked again.

Scott? Scott O'Connor? How could there be any rumors about him? He was such an honest guy. She forced herself to read the allegation concerning the red Porsche he'd brought to school at the beginning of his junior year. Too many people were wondering how he had been able to buy such an expensive car.

"All my rumors are about basketball players," she said, desperately trying to think of a way to get out of investigating Scott.

"I've got football," said the guy who'd covered the team last fall.

"Wrestling and gymnastics for me," Chet reported.

"Would you like to trade?" Sam inquired. When Chet glanced at her curiously, she explained. "You usually work with the men's basketball program, so I thought you might know more about these stories."

"Thanks, but I've got a killer class schedule this semester," Chet told her with a heavy sigh. "Mark's giving me a break on assignments at least until after midterms."

"Don't you want the basketball stories?" Mark asked. "I thought you'd jump at the chance to do a major assignment. After all, you're the one who wanted to do investigative reporting. Right?"

"Right." Sam decided she had to tell Mark the truth. "I just think I might have a conflict of interest."

"Oh, really?" Mark raised his eyebrows, and the other guys turned toward her.

"Well, one of the girls on the basketball team lives down the hall from me at Rogers."

"And . . ." Mark prompted.

"This girl and I have talked about how much she'd like to be a starting player." Sam wasn't comfortable admitting much more about Jean's frustrations with the women's team.

"And you think you might not treat Deb Wilson fairly in order to help the girl move up to a starting position?" Mark asked.

"Of course I'd be fair," Sam replied hastily. Then she realized she had just destroyed one of her reasons for not covering the basketball stories.

"Do you really have a problem, Hill?" Mark inquired. "Or do you just not want to work this hard?"

"It's not a question of how much time the project will take," Sam hedged.

"Look, why don't you just be straight with us? You can't do one of these stories because you're dating Scott O'Connor." Mark's tone was final, saying he didn't want to hear any more weak excuses.

"I'm not sure you could call it dating."

"Spare us the definition of your relationship," Mark said without a hint of sympathy. "Are you afraid that you might discover he's not exactly Mr. Clean?"

Sam was upset by Mark's disregard for the truth about her and Scott: They were friends and maybe a little more than that, but it was too early to say they had a relationship. Mark wasn't giving her a chance to argue the point, but she was determined to convince him she wasn't scared by the possible results of her investigation. "I'm a reporter. I can't worry about what I might discover when I set out to do a story."

"Then what is it?" Mark's brow wrinkled with confusion. "Are you thinking you won't be objective?"

Sam stared at the floor. He'd hit her concern right on the nose, but she hated to admit she wasn't sure she could turn in a story that proved the rumors about Scott were true.

"Sam, you haven't been working with us long, but I think I know one thing about you." Mark's gruff voice seemed to soften a bit. "You're a good reporter, and good reporters separate their personal interests from their stories."

"Thanks, but . . ." Sam appreciated his confidence in her, even if she wasn't sure whether or not she could stay objective.

"Don't wimp out on me, Hill." He was back to his businesslike tone. "We need you around here with Chet having to cut back his time. No one else can do your work for you, so you're going to have to pull it off, no matter what."

She smiled at Mark. He wasn't going to compliment her twice in the same afternoon, but she appreciated the encouragement he'd offered her in that one soft moment; she was going to need all the support she could get to survive her investigations.

"Sorry I couldn't see you last night," Scott said, falling into step beside Sam as she left her child development class.

"I was still catching up on some homework that was left from the weekend," she told him.

He tugged on her long hair. "Does that mean you didn't miss me?"

She hadn't thought of much else besides Scott, but Sam couldn't tell him she had spent the evening wrestling with her conscience about doing a story on him. She shrugged. "I guess you crossed my mind once or twice."

"I had to take my car into Hawthorne Springs to get it looked at," he explained.

The Porsche. Sam's heart skipped a beat, and she tried to stay cool. "Is there someone in town who works on foreign cars?"

"No." He laughed. "I picked up a little dent somewhere, so I took it to a body shop in town for an estimate."

"That's too bad. It's such a beautiful car." His proud smile made Sam feel terrible; already she was trying to get information out of him. But she couldn't help herself—she had to know. "How long have you had it?"

"Since the summer after my sophomore year," he answered.

"It's quite a car for a sophomore to buy." Sam knew she had to find out how he had gotten the car, but she couldn't just ask him right out. "Is your dad so rich he owns all of Lexington or something?"

"Hardly." He stopped by a bench set back a couple feet from the sidewalk. Taking her hand, he led her to sit beside him. "It's kind of embarrassing. My grandmother died that summer and she left me a lot of money."

"That's nice," Sam said, trying to stifle her sigh of relief. "I mean, I'm sorry about your grandmother. But it's nice that she thought so much of you. I don't have any relatives who would leave me anything more than some costume jewelry."

"The funny thing is," Scott said, "no one knew she had all that money, and I certainly never thought of myself as her favorite heir. I thought I was dreaming when Brad Smothers, her lawyer, said it was all mine."

At the same time she was filing away Mr. Smothers' name, Sam could see Scott bringing cookies and magazines to his elderly grandmother. "I bet you took good care of her."

"I used to visit her whenever I could, but I didn't expect her to leave me all that money just because I sat on the porch with her and listened to her stories about the old days. Anyway, I guess I felt pretty funny about the money. Instead of doing something smart like saving it or investing it, I wanted to spend it."

"So you bought the Porsche," Sam concluded.

"Yeah." Scott shook his head, and Sam could almost feel his discomfort. He was embarrassed he'd blown the money on something as flashy as a Porsche 911.

He told her more about his grandmother and his family as they walked to their next class. As they parted to go to separate buildings, Scott told Sam that he'd see her that night.

Sam was humming to herself on her way to Bains Hall and her European history class. She couldn't have asked for a better resolution to her problem than Scott's logical explanation for the car.

Suddenly a pair of strong arms reached out and grabbed her shoulders. "Sam."

She looked up in surprise. "Aaron? What are you doing?"

"We need to talk for a minute," he said, his dark eyes full of concern.

"I'm almost late for class." She wasn't trying to avoid Aaron; she really did have to be there in three minutes.

"I'm too worried about you to let you slip away," he said ominously. "What's happened to you? How can you be seen around campus with Scott O'Connor when the *Herald*, which you now work for, is doing research on NCAA violations?"

Sam was tempted to say Scott always spoke highly of Aaron, and that she didn't appreciate the tone he used when he mentioned Scott's name. "I don't see the problem," she told him instead.

"No?" Aaron dropped one hand, but held tightly to her other arm. "Haven't you heard that he was going to leave Hawthorne after his sophomore year because he didn't think they let him play enough ball?"

His question reminded Sam of the clipping she'd read from an Atlanta paper; it had hinted that Scott was dissatisfied enough at Hawthorne to talk to other schools. "I've heard he wanted to be a starter on the team. That's a reasonable goal for a good athlete."

"Don't be blind." Aaron waved his free hand in her face. "How can you ride around in that glow-in-the-dark Porsche that the coaches used to bribe him to stay at Hawthorne?"

"You think the coaches gave him the car?" Sam was stunned by Aaron's intense interest in the matter. Had he always been that wrapped up in issues? Or was he unusually interested in Scott?

"How else would he get it? Everyone knows he's at Hawthorne on a basketball scholarship. His family isn't wealthy."

"How do you know so much about him?" she queried. "Don't you have better things to do than worry about someone else's car?"

"I swear you're not the same person I used to know," Aaron said. "Your brain has turned to mush. You don't care about anything important anymore. And I think it started when you got stuck with that freshman hippie for a roommate."

"Angie's a good person." Sam was really tired of people knocking her roommate. Although Aaron had helped Angie out when a teacher tried to seduce her, he had never been able to understand her. He said she cared more about animals and trees than people.

Aaron reached out and tapped the "Save the Monkeys" pin on Sam's jacket lapel. "This is just what I mean. I guess it's too much to expect you to see the truth about your new boyfriend."

"He's not my boyfriend!" Sam felt that she was insisting there was nothing between her and Scott every time she turned around.

Aaron shook his head. "There's nothing sadder than an intelligent person who has been brainwashed."

"Good-bye, Aaron," she said firmly.

His sad eyes made Sam's stomach knot. He didn't wish her well or say anything else; he turned away and buried his hands in his jacket pockets. He hunched forward as he walked away, and Sam recognized the slumped posture as a sign of his distress.

Considering the past they had shared, Aaron's criticism really hurt. Maybe he thought he was trying to do her a service by forcing her to face reality, but she didn't agree with his idea of the truth. He was much too willing to accept the lies about Scott. Why? Why would someone as fair as Aaron believe all the stories? Was it possible he was acting so strangely because it hurt him to see her with Scott?

Sam's head was spinning as she walked to the Student Union and got a Coke at the Eatery. She found an empty table and sat down to examine her thoughts; it was no use for her to try to go to history class now. She was too busy thinking about her own history—with Aaron.

On their final night together last summer, they had talked about how hard it would be for them to see each other when they got back to campus. Both had thought it would be especially difficult if one of them started dating someone new. But they had survived a full semester, and Sam had finally gotten to the point where she could be in the same room with him and not be overwhelmed by painful memories. But despite all their strong feelings for each other, Sam couldn't quite believe Aaron was acting out of jealousy.

If Aaron hadn't been trying to convince Sam to stop seeing Scott because he still cared for her, then Aaron had to actually think the rumors were true. Sure, it *was* odd that Scott had returned to school with the car after all the rumors that he would transfer unless he saw more playing time. There might have been people at Hawthorne who didn't expect Scott to come back to campus that fall, and when he showed up in that flashy car everyone must have noticed him.

Sam wished she hadn't run into Aaron. Scott's story had sounded so plausible, but she had to wonder if his grandmother really had died and left him all that money shortly after his frustrating sophomore season. It sounded a little bit convenient.

Convenient? Sam was shocked by her own thoughts. Of course Scott would rather still have his grandmother than have the car. How could she start doubting him just because of Aaron? Aaron hadn't seen Scott's acute embarrassment when he admitted he'd done something as foolish as spending his inheritance on a car. As Sam sipped her soda, she realized she'd fallen victim to Aaron's powers of persuasion.

He really knew how to make an argument for something when he wanted to. The question was, why did he want to convince her that Scott was guilty? And what kind of friend was she to Scott if she could *let* Aaron convince her?

Chapter 9

Sam waited until the girls finished practice and headed toward their locker room. "Coach Mathers, could we talk for a moment?" When the woman squinted at her, Sam realized she should introduce herself. "My name is Samantha Hill, and I work for the *Herald*."

"That was a good piece you wrote about the team," the coach said. "Let's talk in my office."

"Thanks." The test article Sam had written about the girls' team had run in Monday's paper. Since she'd written a general story on the team's goals for the season, Mark had saved it as filler to be used during a slow sports week.

The coach sat down behind her desk and flipped through a stack of phone messages. Sam stood behind the chairs on the student side of the desk. Considering the reason for her visit, she preferred to stay on her feet.

"Did you know the *Herald* is looking into the effect of NCAA rules on sports here at Hawthorne?" she asked, trying to start out the interview in a nonthreatening manner.

"I saw the editorial," Coach Mathers said with a nod, pausing to read one of her messages a second time.

"A lot of people worry about money changing hands when they talk about NCAA rules, but I think grades could be a more common problem. Have you noticed any girls having trouble with the minimum grade point average?"

The coach put down her messages and gave Sam her full attention. "I've got a good group of girls this year. Not only are we going to take first place in the conference, but they're all doing very well in their classes."

"Really? None of your freshmen have had difficulties adjusting to college classes?" Sam asked.

"Just because the girls are athletes doesn't mean they're stupid." The coach leaned forward over her desk. "After reading your article, I thought you knew better than to believe that old stereotype."

"I didn't mean that at all," Sam insisted. "It's well known that a certain percentage of the freshman class had problems with their grades first semester. It makes sense," she added. "College life can be a big change."

The coach relaxed. "That may be true about the general student population, but I saw all my freshmen's grades. They were perfectly acceptable."

Sam pretended to scribble something in her spiral notebook. "Good. And none of the upperclassmen have fallen victim to the legendary killer classes?" Sam listed some of the courses known to have ruined a few grade point averages. "Physics? Biochemical engineering? Advanced accounting? American literature?"

The coach sucked in her breath for a mere second at Sam's mention of the literature class. If Sam hadn't been watching her carefully, she would have missed it.

"Those are difficult classes," Coach Mathers allowed. Then she shook her head. "However, I haven't seen any grade reports that show my girls having problems with any of them."

Sam looked the coach straight in the eyes, and the woman stared right back at her. Writing down notes about her suspicions, Sam mumbled, "Glad to hear it."

The coach stood and prepared to escort Sam out of her office. "Can I assume you're talking with all the coaches about the minimum grade requirement?"

"I'm not sure how the other reporters are handling the sports they've been assigned," Sam said, worried about Coach Mathers' suspicious question. "You see, we've split up the work."

The coach fixed a steely gaze on Sam. "I see."

Sam didn't stick around to find out how much the coach really did understand about her research. She backed out of the office and muttered, "Thanks for your time."

" . . . and then he asked if he could copy my work!" Roni hooted, finishing up her latest story about the guys she was experimenting with in her chemistry class. Instead of finding a personal tutor, her most recent candidate had turned out to be a sponge.

"Imagine copying Roni's notes," Maddie said across the dining table, and all the girls burst into laughter. Roni's grades in science were infamous.

"One more guy to cross off the list as a possible date for the January Bash," Stacy said. "That leaves us with one—no, two—more prospects. And they're both freshmen!"

Roni groaned. "I refuse to go on a date with somebody who's shorter *and* younger than I."

Maddie sighed. "Roni, you can always go with me."

"Is this a private party?" The question came from above them, and all four girls looked up—and up.

"Hi, Scott." Sam had been relaxing with her friends after her unfriendly and unsatisfactory interview with Coach Mathers, but she certainly wouldn't mind including Scott. "I think we were sharing some girls-only miseries, but you're welcome to join us."

To everyone's surprise, he pulled a chair over

from the next table and squeezed in next to Sam. "So what are we discussing?"

"We're just celebrating making it halfway through another week," Roni told him.

"Do you have rough schedules this semester?" he asked sympathetically.

Roni shared her worries about chemistry while sparing Scott the details of her failed plan to find a man. The others told him things were pretty average for them—they were in way over their heads with work. Scott laughed and said he knew how they felt.

He turned to Sam. "That's why I was looking for you. Do you ever go to the midweek movies in the Student Union?"

To celebrate Wednesdays, the Campus Life Council had started sponsoring videotaped movies which were played on the big screen TV. Sam had always been too busy to go, but tonight the idea of getting her mind off her class assignments and the NCAA series of articles was appealing.

"No, I haven't gone yet. Are they showing something good tonight?"

"Only one of my favorite movies of all time," he assured her. "*Hoosiers*."

Sam moaned. *Hoosiers* was a movie about a small high school basketball team in Indiana. "I should have known."

"Since you're so excited," he said with a twinkle in his eye, "would you like to go with me?"

Sam knew she wouldn't have cared if he had invited her to a monster-returning-from-the-dead flick: She would still want to watch it with him. In fact, a scary movie might have been a better deal because she could have reached for his hand in the gory parts.

"Does the blank look on your face mean you don't want to be my date?" he asked, peering into her face.

Date? Scott O'Connor was honestly asking Sam out, and she was being such a fool that he thought she didn't want to go with him. "I'd love to go!"

"I thought you might be getting tired of basketball. If you don't want to see the movie, I'll understand."

"I'd really like to see it." He raised his eyebrows at Sam's insistence, and she quickly searched for a reason she would be anxious to see *Hoosiers* with him. "I'm kinda homesick, Scott. Maybe seeing the Indiana countryside in the movie will remind me of Illinois."

He smiled. "Well, I'm always pleased to help out a homesick sophomore. The movie starts in ten minutes."

Sam had to ask her friends to take a few books back to the suite for her, and then she left with Scott. She should have realized that every Hawthorne basketball player would be at the movie. They had saved some seats in the front, and several arms waved when she and Scott came into the room. Scott chose the two empty seats in the front row, and Sam found herself sitting between Scott and Tom Moore—the two subjects of her investigations. What had seemed like a diversion from her work had suddenly turned into a very uncomfortable situation. Sam slumped down in her chair and hoped the movie would start soon.

"Watching them play that tournament game made me thirsty," Scott declared as the credits rolled and the room was flooded with light. "Would you like to get something to drink?"

"Just you and me?" Sam asked.

"Ooh! A date!" the guys behind them called.

Sam blushed.

Scott leaned down and whispered, "The guys too much for you?"

"They take a little getting used to," she replied, trying to ignore the continuing comments from the guys around them.

He laughed and put his arm around her shoulder. "I know what you mean. Let's go."

They headed for the Eatery, where Scott ordered nachos and sodas for both of them. Once they were settled at a corner table, Sam realized she didn't know what to say. So far, most of what they had in common involved sports, and she definitely did not want to discuss the basketball team.

"You're quiet tonight," Scott said after they'd snacked in silence for a few minutes. "Aren't you feeling well?"

"I guess I'm a little tired."

"I'll bet you are. If your teachers are anything

like mine, they've been piling on the work lately. Then you've got all your work at the paper . . ."

"Thinking about how much work I have to do makes me feel worse," Sam confessed. "It's better not to think about all my obligations at once."

"It is easier to tackle one thing at a time," he agreed. "Are you working on any of this NCAA stuff?"

She looked up in surprise, hoping he hadn't heard too much about the series. "Yeah."

"Really?" His eyes lit up with interest. "What are you researching?"

Sam shifted uneasily in her seat. Stalling for time, she coughed and cleared her throat. "It's confidential."

"I understand," he said, reaching for her hand. "A lot of the athletes are close friends. Mark's probably told all of you to be careful about talking to anyone."

She loved the feel of his strong hand over hers, but there was more than a hint of guilt in her heart. Scott was being considerate because he thought she might be investigating some of his friends. He had no idea she'd been assigned to his story—or that anyone was investigating him at all.

"Hey, are you busy tomorrow?"

"What time tomorrow?"

"Anytime."

"Well, I've got classes all morning. Then I've got to check in at the newspaper office before I cover the water polo match. But I should have some free time after dinner. That is, if no one assigns an extra fifty pages of reading tomorrow."

"Would you consider studying with me?"

Sam gulped. "What's going on? Do you have a big test coming up?"

"It's more like Friday is coming up," he told her finally. "Some pro scouts will be at the game. It's all I can think about."

"So you want to play on a professional team some day," Sam concluded.

"You're a smart kid. No wonder Mark has you on his staff," Scott teased. "Seriously, I'm trying to keep busy. If I spend too much time alone thinking about it, I'm going to get all worked up and play a lousy game."

"I'm flattered that you want me to help keep you busy," Sam said with a smile. Scott seemed like such a confident, poised person that it surprised Sam to learn that the scouts had him rattled. Still, there had to be dozens of girls on campus who would be glad to help him get his mind off the game, and he had chosen her. Sam grinned with delight.

"Mark, I've only got half an hour before the water polo match," she told him impatiently. He'd been flirting with the new typist for the last ten minutes.

"What is it you need?" he asked, rolling his worn chair back to his own desk.

"I've been working on the NCAA stuff, and I want to go over what I've found so far."

Mark motioned for Sam to join him on his side of the desk. Apparently, he wanted to keep the projects top secret. Sam explained Coach Mathers' strange reaction to her questions and told Mark she thought the girls' basketball coach had been lying to her. Next she repeated Scott's story about how he came to own the red Porsche. Finally, she admitted that if Tom Moore was getting money from someone to finance his trips home, then it was being covered very well.

"It looks like Deb Wilson is your best bet right now," Mark decided. "Why don't you talk to her American lit professor and see what you can come up with?" He paused and fixed a serious stare on Sam. "You know, you're going to have to verify O'Connor's story before you can write anything."

Sam nodded, queasy at the thought of going behind Scott's back to either verify his story or disprove it. "What about Tom Moore? The fact that no one knows anything makes me suspicious."

"You're right. He almost sounds *too* clean." He tucked Sam's notes back in her folder. "Do you think you could have the Wilson piece ready for Monday's edition?"

"The series debut?" Sam's heart skipped a beat.

Mark adjusted his glasses. "With what we've got so far, it looks like your story and one of the football stories are the only ones even close to being resolved."

Sam wondered why each time she thought

Mark might be patting her on the back, the compliment turned out to be a matter of scheduling convenience instead. If her stories were good, she wished he would admit it, at least once.

"By the way, I like your cover," Mark said with a grin.

"Pardon me?"

He pointed at her "Save the Monkeys" button. "If you've been wearing that on your interviews, you're probably catching your victims unaware. I bet they think you're some kind of harmless flake."

"There's nothing flaky about this campaign," she told him indignantly.

"Mm-hm." Mark nodded. "Right."

Just to spite Mark, Sam stopped at the features desk on her way out of the office to explain the chimpanzee project to one of the reporters. There was no guarantee the reporter would call Angie, or that the paper would run the story, but Sam felt virtuous for doing her part to help her roommate prove that caring about animals wasn't "flaky."

Chapter 10

The professor's office was at the end of the hall in the English department. Sam knocked gently on the door.

"Yes?"

She opened the door and peeked inside. "Ms. Harper, I'm Sam Hill from the *Herald*. May I have a few moments of your time?"

The woman lifted her head and looked at Sam. "Right now?"

Sam knew it was rude of her to barge in when the teacher was obviously working. "Whenever it's convenient for you. Could I make an appointment for sometime tomorrow?"

"It's all right, you don't need an appointment," she said cheerfully. "I've been grading papers for two hours straight, and I could use a break."

All the chairs in the office were filled with books and photocopied notes, so Sam stood next to the desk and flipped her notebook open to a blank page.

"What are you working on, Sam?" Ms. Harper asked.

"I'm on the sports staff, and we're doing a series of articles on NCAA rules and their application here at Hawthorne," she explained.

"I don't coach any sports," she explained, looking truly confused by Sam's presence in her office.

"Minimum grades are a part of the package," Sam hinted, but the expression on the teacher's face grew more blank. She figured that if subtle comments weren't going to draw any information out of the woman, maybe the direct approach would be more successful. "Let me be frank, Ms. Harper. There are stories circulating about some athletes who have failed your American literature class."

"To be honest," the teacher replied, "not many athletes sign up for that class. As you know, it's an advanced course in the department's program. Not many football players are English majors."

"What about members of the girls' basketball team?" Sam asked boldly. Sam had a feeling she would learn more from Ms. Harper than she had from Coach Mathers.

"I've had a couple of them in my classes in the last few years. None of them failed," she said.

"No one last semester?" Sam inquired. The teacher shook her head.

Sam wondered if the story was false; maybe Deb Wilson had earned a passing grade. Then she remembered that the NCAA rule required athletes maintain a 2.0 grade point *average*. Deb wouldn't have to have actually failed the class to lose her eligibility.

"Could you tell me what grade Deb Wilson earned in your class?" Sam wasn't sure it was an allowable question, but she had to try.

"Grades are confidential," the professor hedged, and Sam thought she was going to have to give up on this source, too. Then Ms. Harper added, "But since it's probably a matter of record, I can tell you her grade was a . . . D."

The slight hesitation combined with the way the teacher suddenly looked down at her desk before announcing the grade made Sam wonder if she had actually heard the truth. A D could have bumped Deb Wilson's GPA below the limit, but Sam didn't think it was enough. She wondered if Ms. Harper had more to say on the subject.

"Thanks for telling me," she told the teacher. "I assume the NCAA has these rules because they know that some athletes get through college without learning much. Do you agree?"

"Yes. It helps the teachers a great deal. Before the rules, a lot of the players didn't even bother to come to class."

Sam shook her head. "Since not everyone who

wants a college education is able to get one, it's a shame some people waste theirs."

"That's true," the teacher said firmly. "I wouldn't be spending my time planning classes and grading papers if I didn't believe that my job was important."

Sam had done her best to prick Ms. Harper's conscience, and all she could do now was wait and see if the teacher had something to admit about Deb Wilson. Sam closed her notebook and prepared to leave. "I appreciate the time you've given me. If you think of anything else that would help me with my article, you can leave a message for me at the *Herald* office." Sam hated to face Mark empty-handed, but it didn't look like the story was going to break before her deadline.

"Miss Hill," the teacher called as Sam started for the door. Ms. Harper stood and clasped her hands behind her back. "It seemed right at the time, but you've made me rethink my decision. Deb Wilson's grade should have been an F. She knew it, and she convinced Coach Mathers to talk to me. Changing the grade to a D so Deb would have a two point zero GPA seemed like the right thing to do for the school. The coach almost made it sound patriotic. But it was wrong then, just as it is wrong for me to continue lying about it now."

"May I use this information?" Sam felt that she was listening to a confession.

"Yes," Ms. Harper said wholeheartedly. "I'm going to Dean Peters with the story as soon as you leave. By the time the paper comes off the presses, the lie will be out in the light."

"I hope Dean Peters appreciates your honesty," Sam said as she reached for the doorknob. She didn't want to get Ms. Harper in trouble.

"Let's hope he believes in better late than never," the teacher said, managing a half-smile.

"How did you like the water polo match?" Scott asked after welcoming her into his dorm room.

"I missed the first half," she said, trying to get a good look around the room. It was certainly much neater than what she had expected from a jock.

Scott took Sam's book out of her arms and set them on the end of his bed. "So that's why you weren't there when I stopped by the pool."

"Spying on me?"

"I wouldn't call it spying. I just wanted to see you."

Sam knew she liked Scott, and she could feel the physical electricity between them, but she wasn't ready for anything hot and heavy to happen. She took a deep breath and told herself to calm down. After all, she'd been alone with Scott in Atlanta, and everything had gone well. She lingered by the door and waited for Scott to make the next move.

"I didn't invite you here to stand around," he said with a smile.

"What exactly did you have in mind?" she asked.

He hurried over and took her by the elbow. "Hey, Sam. Are you wondering if I lured you up here for some immoral purpose?"

Sam thought he made her concerns sound ridiculous. "I guess not."

His free hand came up under her chin and tipped her head back so she had to face him. "You *are* uncomfortable being alone with me."

"Well, you know what kind of reputation most of the football and basketball players have," she said, attempting to keep the situation light.

"Samantha Hill, I thought you'd know better than to listen to rumors," Scott joked. "Being such a factual reporter and all."

He had no idea how deeply that comment hurt Sam. She didn't want to listen to certain rumors about him, but she had to pay attention to them if she planned to complete her next assignment for Mark. In fact, tomorrow morning she was planning on making some phone calls to his home town in Kentucky.

"Lighten up," he said quietly, giving her a quick hug as his arm slid around her back. "I'm working at the desk, and I thought you could set up camp on my bed. Don't wince, it's simply the name of a piece of furniture in this room," he said with a smile. "If you prefer, you can use my desk."

"I'm sorry," Sam said, hurrying to apologize as she realized her imagination had been working overtime. "Guess this day's been so crazy that I'm not thinking straight."

"I know exactly how you feel. No matter how

hard I try not to think about it, I can't get those scouts off my mind," he told her.

"Then why don't we talk about them?" Sam sat on the edge of the bed and shrugged out of her bulky cardigan sweater. Scott pulled up his desk chair so they were nearly knee to knee.

"You sounded surprised yesterday when I said I was worried about the scouts' opinion of me. What did you think I wanted to do after college?"

"I don't even know what your major is," she admitted. In all the clippings Sam had looked at, she hadn't found anything about his academic interests: Was it any wonder the NCAA worried about star collegiate athletes? Nobody cared what or if they were studying, not even the reporters.

"Business." Scott pointed to the books and calculator on his desk. "I'm suffering through advanced statistics this semester."

"So you'll probably be talking with the employers who set up on-campus interviews in the spring," Sam concluded.

"Nope. More than anything, I want to be playing basketball somewhere next year," Scott confessed. His eyes lit up as he thought of his future career in professional sports.

"Then why did you choose such a difficult major, and why are you suffering through advanced statistics?" Sam knew Scott was a responsible person, but there was such a thing as overkill.

"I thought a business background would help

me manage all the money I hope to make."

"Naturally," Sam managed to say before they both burst out laughing. "It could happen. You're smart to be prepared," she told him after they had calmed down a little.

In Sam's past, guys hadn't confided in her until there was some kind of commitment between them. She figured Scott had to have some amount of trust in her or he wouldn't be discussing his concerns for his future so openly. The idea that she could be special to Scott thrilled her, but Sam wondered if she was reading too much into things. Was it possible Scott really cared about her?

It surprised Sam to consider Scott might be thinking of her as more than just a good friend. Her own feelings about him had been so wrapped up in her inexplicable crush on him that she hadn't asked herself how she really felt about Scott. She'd fallen for him the first time she saw him, and she liked everything she had discovered about him since then. But she'd been too busy to stop and reassess her feelings. Had she progressed from her high-school level infatuation?

"Sam, are you thinking about my career or have you left me for the planet Mars?" Scott asked politely.

"Sorry." Sam shook her head to clear it. "You made me start thinking about some other things. But I don't want to talk about them. I want to talk about tomorrow's game. How do you feel about it?"

"Being a senior, I want to make plans for next year and the years after that, but I know I can't control how the game will go tomorrow night. I hope I play well. But even if I do, I don't know what the pro scouts will put in their reports about me or what will happen in the draft in the spring."

Sam reached out for his hand, and he stretched out his arm to meet her halfway. "All you can do is play your best tomorrow night," she said softly.

"That's not much," he said impatiently, and Sam could tell he was holding back a lot of nervous energy.

"I don't agree," she challenged him. "I think your best is pretty impressive."

"Is that your professional opinion as a sports reporter?"

Sam smiled when she remembered how smoothly he could move down the court, stealing the ball and making an impossible basket. "Definitely."

He heaved a sigh. "I just wish there were more I could do. I wish I could arrange things to be the way I want them to be."

"You remind me of someone I used to know," Sam said, thinking back to her high school boyfriend, Jon.

"Is that good or bad?" he asked. Cocking his head, he tried to read the emotions in her eyes.

"When I first came to Hawthorne, I was still going out with the guy I dated all through high school." Sam stopped to find the right words to describe Jon. "He was an expert arranger. He had planned both of our futures. But when I got here his plans didn't work for me."

"What about him? After he gave up planning your life did he stay in control of his own? Is it possible to arrange your own future?"

"I suppose things are going his way—but Jon would do anything to make his plans happen." She remembered how hard he'd tried to make her come back to him after things had blown up between her and Aaron. It seemed as though Jon would use anyone and do anything to make things turn out the way he'd planned they would. In fact, if Jon were in Scott's position, he would be twisting her arm right now, trying to make her help him somehow with the big game. As a joke Sam said, "You know, tomorrow night I could use my press credentials to get an interview with the scouts. And it would only be natural if I mentioned your name a few times and—"

"No!" Scott interrupted. "Don't you dare!"

"I was just kidding," she said quickly. She took a second to think over his adamant refusal. "If I had been serious, what would be so terrible about my helping you a little bit?" she asked.

"Maybe your old boyfriend didn't mind favors, but I have to do this on my own," he insisted. "If I'm not good enough to be on a professional team, then I don't deserve any scout's attention."

"That's admirable."

"No, it's practical," he corrected. "I'd just be wasting a lot of time, not to mention embarrassing myself, if I made a fool of myself at a tryout."

Sam nodded, impressed once again with Scott's philosophy. He had hopes for his future, and he wanted them to come true just as much, if not more, than Jon did. But whereas Jon didn't particularly care how the future became a reality, Scott had principles. He cared about people, and he cared about living his life honestly. And what was amazing to Sam was how easily she could relate to Scott's philosophies!

She wanted to share her realization that Scott—not the handsome image she'd first fallen for, but the real person—was very special; but she didn't have the nerve to tell him how she felt—not yet. It was hard to believe she had to make those calls to Lexington tomorrow morning to check out his story. Sam tried to put that job out of her mind.

"Almost midnight," he announced after they had spent an hour or so talking about their families and their close friends. "Coach's curfew."

"You're not serious," she responded. Scott didn't strike her as the kind of guy who would actually have a curfew. After all, he was a senior, not a freshman.

"Really, Sam. The night before a game, Coach Tupper wants us to have lights out at midnight."

She almost told him she wouldn't care if he turned out the lights. But instead she asked, "Does the coach do bed checks?"

"That would be cute, " Scott agreed. "But he trusts us to follow his lights-out rule."

Sam didn't have to be told that Scott willingly followed the rule. Even when there were no pro scouts coming to the game, he wanted to play his best. Most Thursday nights, he probably got in bed by eleven, just to be sure he'd be in top form the next day. Some people might laugh at his dedication, but Sam loved it. He was predictable, but in a good way. He was never boring, at least, not to Sam.

"Well, I'll be going, then, so you won't have to lie to Coach Tupper tomorrow." Sam picked up her sweater off the bed.

Scott held the cardigan out so she could slip her arms into the sleeves. "A smart move, Hill. Otherwise, I would have to tell him that the *Herald's* newest sports reporter was leading me astray. He'd probably ban you from the gym."

She grabbed her books and hurried to the door. "How would I ever explain that to Mark?"

"Don't run off too fast," he suggested, walking slowly toward the door. "I really appreciate your hanging out with me tonight. You never touched the work you brought over. I hope you won't be in any trouble tomorrow."

"Tomorrow's Friday," she said with a shrug. "I can catch up over the weekend."

"Not if I have anything to say about it." He moved closer and slid his hand around the back of her neck. "I'd like to spend some time with you."

"I'm sure it can be arranged—" Sam had more to say, but Scott suddenly leaned down to kiss her. His lips pressed against her mouth softly at first, but the kiss grew more insistent before either of them realized what was happening.

Suddenly Scott pulled back and took a deep breath.

"I guess it's a good thing the coach has a curfew," Sam said with a shy smile.

"I only meant to kiss you good night. Honest." he insisted.

"In that case, I'll just say good night." If Sam stayed any longer, there was a chance they would both give into temptation and break Coach Tupper's rule.

"Maybe I should walk you back to Rogers," he said.

"You don't need to." Sam could imagine another kiss on the dorm steps that would have all the girls talking and make Scott late for his curfew.

"Yes, I do." He reached into his closet for his letter jacket. "What kind of guy makes his girlfriend walk home alone in the middle of the night?"

Sam wasn't about to argue with Scott's Sir Galahad act—not when he had actually called her his girlfriend!

Chapter 11

"You're home late," Angie said with a good-natured smile when Sam tried to sneak into the room.

"Hmm . . ."

"Sounds like you had quite a night." Angie was sitting up in bed with the covers draped around her waist.

"It was nice," Sam said dreamily.

"Roni said you were studying with Scott O'Connor." When Sam didn't reply, Angie went on. "I can't imagine studying with him around. He'd be much too distracting."

"Angie Perelli, are you asking me what went on tonight in Scott's room?" Sam was surprised that her nature-conscious roommate was so interested in her potential romance.

"You were in his room? Alone with him?"

"Would you believe me if I said the whole basketball team was there with us?" Sam teased Angie.

"Not for a minute, Ms. Hill." Angie shook her finger at Sam. "Are you going to tell me the truth?"

"Honestly, Angie, we just talked. He's got some things on his mind that he needed to discuss."

"And that's what has you dreamy eyed and flustered?"

Sam kneeled on the floor next to Angie's bed and kicked off her shoes. "I think he likes me," she whispered.

"And that's why your cheeks are all flushed?" Angie asked when she got a closer look at Sam's face.

"No," Sam said with a smile. "I think that's because he really knows how to kiss."

Angie rolled her eyes toward the ceiling. "You're hopeless."

Sam felt her cheeks growing even warmer. "Give me a break."

"All right," Angie agreed with a sigh. "It's just that everyone was wondering about you and Scott, and I got curious."

"You mean you were waiting up for me?" Sam thought she had outgrown that routine when she left her parents for Hawthorne.

"I hate to disappoint you, but I was making some notes for my interview tomorrow." Angie lifted a piece of paper from the blanket.

"You're interviewing someone?" Sam was confused. "Is it a class project or something?"

"No, a girl is coming here to interview me about the chimpanzee protest," Angie corrected. "She's a reporter from the *Herald*—the one you found for me."

"She's doing a story on your campaign?"

"Yeah. Thanks for using your influence." Angie stared at her paper for a minute. "I've got to make a few notes. Will it bother you if I have the light on for a while?"

"Not at all." Sam pulled her turtleneck shirt over her head and reached for the oversized T-shirt she liked to wear around the dorm. "I have to draft a story I finished researching today."

"What dedication!"

"Not dedication." Sam touched her still-warm cheeks. "There's no way I'm going to fall asleep in the next hour, anyway."

The two girls worked quietly with the radio humming in the background. Sam was pretty proud of getting the truth from Ms. Harper, although she would be interested to hear how Dean Peters had reacted to the English teacher's revelation. It wasn't like Sam to be so persistent. The Samantha Hill she knew so well would have been intimidated by the coach and never even tried to face down the teacher. There had been a lot of changes in her thinking and her life during her freshman year, but the changes hadn't stopped happening. She wasn't in a sophomore slump at all. And the new, improved Sam had a chance at a romance with a wonderful guy.

Sam started to outline the article for next week's *Herald*. It would have to include the rumor, the coach's denial, and Ms. Harper's final admission. And if a decision was reached soon enough, she would end the story with the consequences. She knew Deb Wilson would be suspended, but she didn't know if the discipline would cover a few games or last for the rest of the season. Sam wondered what Jean's chances were of winning a starting position from the fiasco.

Mark had been so sure that Sam could remain objective, but she had to examine her unusual persistence once again. Had she pushed so hard to get someone to say Deb Wilson's grade had been altered just because she was prejudiced in Jean's favor? Sam couldn't afford to believe she'd acted out of personal preference, because if she'd done that for Jean, there was no telling what she might do to clear Scott's name.

Sam didn't even bother to get dressed on Friday morning. She could have gone to the *Herald* office to make her calls to Kentucky, but she didn't want to risk an emotional scene in public, especially in front of Mark Malone. She washed her face, made a cup of coffee, and crawled back into bed with a note pad.

She found the area code for Lexington in the Atlanta phone book, and then she dialed directory assistance in the city. Her only lead was the grandmother's lawyer, Brad Smothers. She punched out the number with her index finger.

"Good morning, law office."

"Mr. Smothers, please." Sam's hands were shaking and she stretched out her writing hand, trying to make it come alive before she had to start taking notes.

"Brad Smothers speaking." The man on the other end of the connection spoke with a soft, southern drawl. He sounded nice.

"Hello, Mr. Smothers. My name is Samantha Hill, and I'm calling you from Hawthorne Springs, Georgia." She hated giving out her name in case someone in Lexington knew the O'Connors, but she couldn't expect the lawyer to answer her direct questions if she refused to identify herself.

"What can I do for you on this fine morning, Miss Hill?" he asked.

"I'm in the psychology department of Hawthorne College, and we're doing a survey on student purchasing habits," she lied. "One of the Hawthorne students, a Mr. Scott O'Connor, owns a red Porsche. He says it was his first choice of what to do with money he inherited from his grandmother."

"I remember Bessie willing that money to her grandson. You probably know she died June twenty-ninth two years back. Now just what did you say your question was, dear?"

"Sometimes people's recollections can be fuzzy, and I'm simply trying to verify that the car was honestly the first thing that this student

wanted to buy when he came into some cash."
Sam covered the mouthpiece on the receiver and
took a deep breath.

"Why are you doin' this survey?"

"It's for a big paper the department is writing
up. We want to know what motivates kids to
spend money on certain things—while neglect-
ing others."

"Graduate research?" he inquired.

"Yes, sir. In fact, it will probably be published
by the college," Sam went on. That wasn't exactly
a lie, she thought.

"Okay. Well now, I'm trying to picture the day
the O'Connor family was gathered in my office
for the reading of the will. Everyone was stunned
when Bessie left it all to the young man. As I
remember, he was too astonished to say how he
planned to spend the money."

Sam didn't like the hole his story left in her
research. Mark would say Scott had stashed the
money in some out-of-the-way bank and still
accepted the car from the coaches. "So you don't
know whether he considered any other ways to
invest the inheritance?"

"No. Can't say that I do." He paused to think.
"You might check with Taylor's Sports Cars. For
all I know, they're the ones who talked him into
buying the Porsche. You know how salesmen
are."

"Thank you so much, Mr. Smothers. You have
been very helpful."

"You're most welcome, miss. Maybe I'll see this

conversation in print someday! I wish you luck with the rest of your survey."

As soon as the lawyer hung up his phone, Sam called directory assistance for the number of the sports car dealership.

A sleazy-sounding salesman answered the phone, and Sam adopted a sexy voice that she didn't even know she owned. He warmed up to her immediately and volunteered to find the sales records from two years ago while she waited. Sam knew she was running up a hefty long-distance bill, and she hoped the *Herald* would reimburse her.

"I have the invoices right here, honey," he told her. Sam heard paper crackling at his end of the line.

"Whom does it show as the purchaser?"

"We sold three red Porsche nine elevens in the time you specified. The buyers were Honey Mc-Comb, Ray Bob Jesperson, and Scott O'Connor."

"What details can you find on the O'Connor invoice?" she asked, trying to keep any excitement out of her voice.

He sighed, and it sounded as if he were straightening out a crumpled piece of paper. "He bought the car on August second of the year in question. He had a bank check from Harris Trust Company for the full amount. Hm." He stopped to read more of the sheet, then gave her the car's serial number.

"Is there any indication where the money came from?" she asked, glad to be free of the games she'd had to play with the lawyer. Since this salesman seemed to think she would stop by and see him if she ever set foot in Kentucky, he didn't care what she asked him, or why.

"We don't care where it comes from, unless it's stolen." He laughed hard at his own joke. "Honestly, honey, there's no way to tell from the invoice copy."

"Okay, well, thanks for your help."

"My pleasure, sugar. Just remember to see old Bobby the next time you're in town."

Sam giggled for a minute while she considered her next move. She knew Grandma Bessie had died June twenty-ninth and Scott had driven off with the Porshe on August second. It was no wonder he'd seemed a little embarrassed by the whole affair. He'd barely waited a month to spend his grandmother's money. Sam knew Mark would want more proof that the money from Grandma Bessie was the same money he'd given the car dealer. Sam rubbed her chin and wondered how much information she could get from the Harris Trust Company. She checked the road atlas her brothers had given her last Christmas— so she could find her way home if necessary— and came up with her next scheme.

"Harris Trust Company? This is Dora with the Fayette County Auditor's Division," she said, trying to mimic Scott's Kentucky accent.

"What can I do for you today, Dora?" asked the woman in customer accounts.

"I'm trying to track the activity in the account of one Scott O'Connor."

"Account number?"

"The carbon has been smeared, and I'm afraid I can't read it. Can you help me?"

The woman at Harris Trust explained they'd had a busy morning, but there was a lull at the moment. She offered to find the account number and pull the records up on her computer terminal. Sam didn't know whether she should be glad for all the cooperation she was getting from strangers: A small part of her was still worried she might find something out she didn't want to know. And the thought that someone could dig into her own past this easily was frightening.

"I've got the record on my screen," the woman announced. "It's account zero nine five, two three seven, five four two nine one."

Sam made a note of the number just to have something to do with her nervous hands. "I'm looking for account activity in late June and early July two years back."

"There was a substantial deposit—fifty-two thousand six hundred ninety dollars to be exact—in his account on June thirtieth. It looks like it was a certified check from another local bank. Then he withdrew almost all that money on August second in the form of a cashier's check. I guess he bought a very nice car with it; the check was made out to Taylor's, which is the most expensive dealership in town."

"Oh, really?" Sam said, hoping her accent

wasn't changing each time she opened her mouth.

"What are you trying to find out, Dora?" the woman asked, as if she expected to hear some juicy gossip in exchange for her favor.

"We're just tracking money exchanges for the tax records," Sam said, inventing the reason as she spoke. She had no idea what kind of taxes they had in Kentucky, and she crossed her fingers hoping the woman would buy her story.

"All I can say is this guy got a windfall and spent it as fast as he could. Makes you wonder how he came by it, huh?"

"I suppose it does. Well, thanks for your help. I owe you a lunch."

Sam hung up before any actual lunch date could be arranged. She still couldn't prove it was the inheritance that had been deposited in the Harris Trust Company account. A skeptical person might suggest Scott could have sheltered his inheritance in a different financial institution, and that the money in Scott's Harris Trust account had come from someone at Hawthorne. Sam told herself she was trying to think like Mark Malone when she looked for the holes in her story; that was easier than thinking the suspicions were her own.

Reviewing the facts, Sam knew the amount of the deposit Scott had made at Harris Trust on June thirtieth. The figure was written in large round numbers on her notepad: $52,690. How could she find out if that total matched the inheritance? The lawyer certainly wasn't going to tell her.

There had to be somewhere else where they recorded settlements and wills in the county. She tried to remember all the people her parents had had to deal with when Grandpa Hill died during her senior year of high school. Sam rubbed her temples, trying to bring the old memories back into focus. The word *probation* kept coming to mind; then she remembered the day her father had to meet with the *probate* judge.

Sam quickly composed another story as she waited for the number from directory assistance

"I'm calling from the Historical Society," Sam told the Fayette County probate clerk when she got the right office. She tried to use her Kentucky accent again. "I'm an intern doing research on the estates of some Fayette County residents who passed away in the last five years."

"If you have a list of persons, you'll have to come in and do the work yourself," the clerk told her firmly.

"I just have one name today, and I've got to go out of town at noon. I'd surely appreciate any help you could offer." Personally, Sam couldn't think of a single reason why this stranger should take time to help her, but she prayed the woman would give her the last piece to her puzzle.

"All right, go ahead. What's the name?"

"Bessie O'Connor. She died June twenty-ninth two years ago."

The clerk set the phone down with a clink and

rustled through some files. Meanwhile, there was a knock on Sam's door, and she hoped whoever it was would go away if she pretended no one was home.

"I have the record here in front of me," the woman declared. "Believe it or not, we were just going to send the records through June thirtieth of that year into storage, and the box was right by my desk."

"This must be my lucky day," Sam commented. The woman in Kentucky had no idea how lucky Sam had been so far.

"Her total estate was valued at sixty-five thousand, two hundred thirty-three dollars.

Sam's stomach sank. The total didn't match the amount of money Scott had deposited at Harris.

"Will that do it?" the clerk inquired.

"That doesn't quite match the figure I have," Sam said, hoping there was some logical explanation.

The knocking at the door grew more insistent and when Sam still ignored it, the door opened a crack and Stacy stuck her head into the room. When she saw Sam on the phone, she mouthed, "Are you sick?"

Sam shook her head vigorously, praying the woman in Kentucky would say she had pulled the wrong file.

"My figure's too high or too low?" the woman asked, sounding more and more impatient.

"It's higher than the one in my files." Sam tried not to pay any attention as Stacy pulled out her desk chair and took a seat. She hoped the probate clerk wouldn't ask what kind of information Sam had in her files at the Historical Society.

"Maybe you have the amount of money left to the family after taxes," the clerk suggested.

"What would that be?" Sam asked, her stomach settling a bit.

"After taxes were paid, the amount delivered to the lawyer was fifty-two thousand, six hundred ninety dollars."

"That's it!" It was impossible for Sam to hide her excitement. She tried to control herself and finish her conversation. "Thanks for the help. Now I can take that vacation without having this file waiting for me on my desk when I get back."

"Have a good time," the woman said glumly as Sam ended the call.

"Files? Vacation? What's going on here?" Stacy demanded. "I heard you skipped your first class, and I was worried you'd come down with the plague."

Sam pressed her palm to her own forehead. "I feel fine to me."

"Roni thought you were sleeping in because you'd had such a hot date with Scott last night," Stacy said, ignoring Sam's theatrics. "What are you doing in bed surrounded with scribbled pieces of paper and making strange calls?"

"Stacy, I have to tell you. I'm working on one of the NCAA investigations," Sam confessed. She told Stacy that Scott was the subject of her morning's phone calls and how awful it made her feel to be following up her story behind his back. "When I'm with him sometimes, I feel like such a rat," she said.

"But you're just doing your job," Stacy said in Sam's defense. "And he's lucky you're the one working on his story. I bet you're working harder to get the true story than anyone else would."

Sam had to admit that was the truth. She had pushed herself to find every clue in the treasure hunt. Now no one, not Mark Malone, not Aaron Goldberg, could say there were questions about where Scott got the money for the car.

"Look at it this way," Stacy continued. "You've been given the chance to put an end to the ugly rumors and clear Scott's name."

"That's right! Why haven't I thought of it that way?" Sam asked.

"I think you've just been too close to the whole thing. I know you were supposed to keep it confidential, but I wish you had talked to me earlier if it was bothering you so much. It might have helped."

"I hate to ask this, but—"

Stacy raised her hand to halt Sam's warning. "My lips are sealed. No one will know about this story until the paper hits the stands."

"Ugh, then everyone will see it, especially Scott." Sam couldn't help worrying.

"And I bet he'll appreciate what you've done for him," Stacy said with authority. Sam hoped with all her heart that her friend was right.

Chapter 12

Sam tried to take a deep breath, but there wasn't enough fresh air in the crowded gymnasium. The band was great and everyone was dancing their hearts out, enjoying the campus council's attempt to banish January doldrums.

"Need some air?" Scott asked, bending close so she could hear him as the band started their next song.

Sam simply nodded, pretty sure he wouldn't hear her answer if she tried to talk. Sam had been planning to go to the dance with all her single friends, but Scott had found her after his victorious performance in the basketball game last night and asked her to be his date: How could she say no?

They had to find their shoes before they could

go outside. The basketball coaches weren't thrilled about dances being held in the gym, so everyone had to remove their shoes before stepping onto the court. This year someone, and Sam suspected it was Tucker Morris, had come up with a shoe-check system. Scott had to pay fifty cents to get their Reeboks out of hock.

The January evening was chilly, and Sam shivered when the air first hit her face. "Are you cold?" Scott asked.

"How could I be?" she asked. "We've been dancing in that sauna for over an hour."

Scott put his arm around her shoulder and pulled her close. "Are you complaining?"

"Not at all." She had seen several heads turn in her direction when she and Scott moved onto the floor and started dancing. Once, during a slow song when she was holding Scott tightly, Erica had looked as if she were ready to kill Sam. Of course, Sam's view was slightly obstructed; her cheek had been pressed against his chest, and she could barely see past his arm.

"Coach Tupper said the scouts like me," he said casually.

"What?" She slugged him in the arm. "Why didn't you tell me sooner?"

"If you remember, you were so busy today that you had to meet me *here*, at the door. We've been surrounded by people ever since then. This is the first chance we've had to talk without screaming."

"You're right." Sam had been having so much

fun dancing with him, holding his hand, and throwing her arms around his neck for the slower songs, that it was hard to believe they hadn't really talked about anything. "Tell me what the scouts said."

"The coach didn't give me a lot of specifics," Scott told her, "but I guess they felt I was a strong all-around player."

"Is that good?"

"Who knows?" Scott shrugged. "Some teams want specialists, others need all-around guys. It all depends on who'll be drafting what kinds of players in the spring."

Sam reached for his hand and squeezed it. "I hope there's a team looking for someone just like you."

"Yeah. That's enough about me, what were you doing all day?"

"Turning in a couple of stories for Monday's paper, working on another article, and trying to get some help with my statistics assignment that's due next week."

"I could help you. I took that class, remember?"

"You'd be saving my life—and my grade point average. I have to do a big project to present to the class on Monday. It would be great if you could explain some stuff to me before then."

"Tomorrow afternoon?" he asked.

"Perfect."

Scott's brow wrinkled, as if he were confused. "Wait a minute—did you say you're not busy tomorrow afternoon? Don't you have to cover something for the paper?"

"There aren't any big sporting events on Sunday," she said. But she knew what he had meant. They would probably be spending a lot more time together if he didn't always have basketball practice and if she wasn't constantly busy with her *Herald* work.

"Don't you have to work on the NCAA thing?"

"No, my projects are going pretty well. I think I can afford to take a few days off," Sam said, trying to stay as calm as possible.

"You have more than one investigation going on?" He seemed truly surprised. "Are there that many rumors of violations?"

"Scott . . ."

He slapped his own face. "I know, it's all confidential. But I've got to admit I'm curious to read your stories."

"I'll have one in Monday's paper, so you won't have to wait too long." Unfortunately, it was looking as if her story on Scott would be ready for the next week. And then what would happen? Sam had to ask herself.

"I sent my family the highlight column you wrote about me," he said, watching her face closely for her reaction. "They liked it. In fact, my mother called this morning to say you were very observant. Not many reporters here try to describe my style of play, they just count up the rebounds, steals, and baskets."

"I'm glad they liked it." Sam liked the idea of

adding a new dimension to the paper's already excellent sports page. She wondered if anyone else had noticed it besides Scott's mother. "Did she call just to talk about the column?"

His face grew serious. "Not really. Her cousin works at a bank in town, and she told my family someone had called the teller in the next booth and asked a lot of questions about my account."

Sam nearly choked. "That's weird," she finally managed to get out.

Scott was too lost in thought to pay much attention to Sam's shocked reaction. "The caller was from the county auditor's office, but I can't imagine why anyone would be checking into my records. It's a creepy feeling."

"I'll bet it is," she mumbled. She'd felt pretty creepy doing it yesterday.

He grabbed her arm and grinned. "But I'd rather dance with you than worry about some auditor in Kentucky. Let's get back inside!"

His sudden enthusiasm was infectious, and Sam smiled up at him, forgetting her worries. "The last one to get their shoes off has to pay to get them back after the dance!" she challenged as she headed back to the gym.

On Sunday night Sam was curled up in bed reading her child development book. Stacy, Roni, Liz, and Maddie had gone to the Eatery for a nine o'clock snack, but Sam didn't want to get out of her cuddly nest and go out into the cold night air. Angie was busy with Tucker in the library plotting next Saturday's demonstration, and the whole floor seemed quiet for once.

The gentle knock on the door surprised her. "Yes?"

Jean Jones stuck her head into the room. "Do you have a minute, Sam?"

Sam closed her book and rearranged her covers. "How are things going with the team?"

Jean leaned against the wall. "You know that Deb Wilson has been suspended for the rest of the semester."

Sam nodded. Ms. Harper had called her with that information after the dean met with the school's athletic director. "Has that changed anything for you?"

"No." Jean didn't sound too frustrated. "Deb was a forward, and Coach Mathers thinks I'm stronger as a defensive player."

"That's too bad. I thought there might be a spot for you on the starting team when I found out Deb Wilson was ineligible."

"It's okay," Jean said sincerely. "I've been thinking a lot about what Scott told me. It's important for me to see myself as a part of the team, even if I'm not a starter. I just do my best whenever I have a chance to help."

"And that's enough?" It surprised Sam that Jean's attitude had turned around so completely.

"It all depends on how you look at things. Each time I get to play in a game, I look at it as an opportunity. The most important thing for me right now is to help the team win. And as Scott says, every time the coach sees me playing my best, she'll realize how much the team needs me."

Sam was amazed by the change in Jean's perspective. Two weeks ago she'd been a frustrated ball player who seemed ready to transfer. She wondered how much of the change in her was due to Scott's pep talk—probably most of it. "Scott does have some good ideas," Sam said.

"And have you seen his slam dunk?" Jean asked, her eyes sparkling with admiration. "He's wonderful."

"That's for sure." So far, Sam hadn't seen a single thing about Scott's personality that she didn't like. She felt like the luckiest girl on campus—in the world. Crossing her fingers, she hoped silently that her luck would hold out over the next few weeks.

Sam was a celebrity the minute the *Herald* hit the stands on Monday. She expected some students to be angry with her over the Wilson story. Normally, no one liked a rat who turned in other people. But Maddie pointed out the good parts of the situation as they stood outside the Student Union, in between classes.

"What would have happened if the story went uncovered until tournament time? Can you imagine how it would look if the team were disqualified because of Deb's cheating?"

"Even if the whole team weren't disqualified, the rest of the girls would be upset, trying to play without her," Sam said, beginning to understand.

"This way, someone can move into Deb's position and the team's conference hopes aren't necessarily gone."

"Can you believe this?" Sam was suddenly struck with how strange the conversation sounded. "Two weeks ago, we didn't know a thing about the girls' basketball team. . . . and we didn't care about our ignorance. Now we're discussing their championship possibilities without Deb Wilson!"

"It's called broadening your horizons," Maddie said with a laugh. "That's what happens when you get involved."

Sam saw Scott striding down the path in her direction. "And that's not the only fringe benefit," she told Maddie with a laugh.

"Really." Maddie shook her head. "I tried out for the play and got a broken heart. You give up men and work for the newspaper, and romance falls in your lap. Sometime you'll have to tell me how you did it."

"Good morning to my favorite reporter," Scott said, brushing Sam's forehead with a soft kiss.

"It's nice to see you, too." Sam said, surprised by his enthusiastic greeting.

"Hi, Scott." Maddie waved at him.

"How are you doing, Maddie?" he asked politely.

"Fine, but I have to . . . Well, I have to do something now. I think it's go to the library. Yeah, I'm sure of it," she said, looking at her books. " 'Bye!"

"See you later!" Sam called after her retreating friend.

Scott produced a copy of the paper from under his arm. It was folded open to Sam's article. "This is really good."

Sam grinned. Scott's praise meant more to her than any of the tributes she'd heard that morning. "Thank you."

"I know Deb pretty well," he told her. "I had no idea she had a grade scam going. What are you sports people going to turn up next?"

"What?" Sam sputtered.

"The introduction to the two reports promises there are more stories to come. I was just wondering how they plan to top this one!"

"I can't—"

"I'm not pumping you for details," Scott insisted. "I'm just so impressed with your work. I can't believe anyone else will do anything as good. How did you manage to dig up the proof?"

Sam's head was swimming with the compliments. Scott set such high standards for himself that she knew he wasn't easily impressed. She was trying to find a way to tell him how much his support meant to her when someone tapped her on the shoulder.

She turned her head to find Aaron standing behind her. Remembering their last encounter, she didn't know what to expect.

"I think your article's great, Sam," Aaron said. "I hope all the stories are handled so responsibly."

Sam knew Aaron was referring to the rumors

concerning Scott. He couldn't possibly know she was the one assigned to that story, so Sam decided to play innocent. "Thanks. I'll be sure to pass along your comments to the rest of the staff."

Aaron gave her an intense look with his dark eyes before he spun around and walked away.

"What was that all about?" Scott asked, shaking his head in confusion.

"It's hard to say," Sam lied. "Sometimes Aaron's so wrapped up in a class or a project that he doesn't quite operate on the same plane as the rest of us."

"That must have made your relationship very interesting." Scott flipped a loose strand of hair out of Sam's face.

Sam reached for his hand and held it tightly. "I guess it was interesting, but I've been having a lot more fun with you—and I've never been bored, believe me."

He rested his hands on her shoulders. "That's nice to know," he said mysteriously.

"Really? Why?"

"Why am I so happy that you like spending time with me?" he teased her.

"Is that why you're happy?" She had no idea where the conversation was leading, but she could spend the rest of her life having him look at her with that tender light in his eyes.

"Samantha, I'm so happy because I've met a woman I wasn't sure even existed." He paused to take a breath. "Sam, I'm falling in love with you."

For months, Sam hadn't been sure she would ever hear those words again—and she certainly hadn't dared hope to hear them from someone as perfect for her as Scott. Tears blurred her vision as she threw her arms around his neck and their lips came together in a delighted kiss.

When it ended, Scott softly kissed the tip of her nose. "Does this mean you feel the same way?" he asked shyly.

Sam hadn't been brave enough to give a name to her growing feelings for Scott, but she knew she was in love with him, too. The time they spent together was magic. He understood her. They cared about each other's goals and supported each other's accomplishments. It was a matter of respect, and she'd never been in a relationship where the partners were so equal. Jon had wanted to run her life. Aaron's dreams had been more important than hers. But Scott valued her opinions and let her make her own choices.

"I know this isn't very romantic, standing in the middle of the campus with people walking past staring at us. But I can't wait, Sam. I have to know how you feel," he whispered urgently.

She stroked his cheek with her palm. "Scott, I'm in love with you, too."

He tangled his fingers in her hair and grinned. "I don't suppose this is the place to really celebrate."

"Do you have something more private in mind?" Sam inquired.

"I wish I did." His face collapsed in a tragic frown. "But I've got a class in five minutes."

Sam checked her watch. "Oh, no. I was supposed to be at the *Herald* office ten minutes ago!"

"No one said this was going to be easy," he said, patting her on the back. "But we can make it work."

Sam loved the confidence in his voice. Of course, he didn't know about the potentially bumpy days ahead, but she told herself he was right. If the investigation bothered Scott, he would give her a chance to explain. No matter what happened, he loved her. They would cruise right through the rough waters.

Chapter 13

"Mind if I get dressed before the interview?" Bart Hanson asked Sam, water dripping off his bare, tanned chest.

"Please do," Sam advised. She wasn't sure she should have thanked Mark Malone for recommending Bart for the athlete-of-the-week column. It was a slow sports week, and he thought it would be a good idea for her to interview the California senior who had single-handedly brought water polo to Hawthorne. But he hadn't mentioned that Bart was exactly the kind of guy Angie was so glad to have left behind on the West Coast.

"Need a bodyguard for this interview?" Scott asked from the doorway.

After Bart disappeared into the locker room,

157

Sam ran over to Scott. The pool area was a little wet, and she had to be careful not to slip. "What are you doing here? I thought you had practice."

"Coach had a faculty meeting and he left us to practice on our own," he told her.

"So you're skipping practice? That doesn't sound like Scott O'Connor."

"What if I said I just *had* to see you?" he asked, raising one eyebrow to test her gullibility.

"I'd say I was a bad influence on you."

"You'd be wrong," he said smugly. "The coach had us call an hour-long captain's practice, so we did, and it's over. And not a moment too soon, from what I saw from the door."

"What did you see?" Bart hadn't been wearing very much, but that's the way the water polo players always looked.

"I saw him eyeing you like a wolf considering the best way to catch a helpless little rabbit."

"Your comparison is charming, but I don't see myself as a helpless rabbit," Sam said with pride.

"Yeah, well, we both know how tough you are. Old Bart should just think about Deb Wilson for a minute, and then he'd know better than to mess with you. Unfortunately, he doesn't look that smart," Scott decided. "Just in case he has some strange ideas about your interview, I think I'll stick around."

The interview went quickly as soon as Bart realized he wasn't going to be able to make a move on Sam. He had no problem talking almost nonstop about himself, giving Sam enough information for her column in ten minutes. After she thanked Bart, she turned and found Scott sitting in the first row of seats.

"Ready for a snack at the Eatery?" he asked, his words echoing in the empty pool area.

"It's only an hour before dinner. It would spoil my appetite," she said automatically.

"You sound like my mother," he complained, stretching his legs before he stood. "But I wouldn't worry about saving your appetite. The menu for tonight is creamed globs on toast."

She covered her face with her hands and moaned. In the entire history of Hawthorne, no one had been able to figure out what the cooks put in the creamy sauce they poured on toast twice a month.

"Does that mean you want to grab a burger with me now?" he asked.

Sam shifted nervously from foot to foot. "I've got an appointment to see someone about an article I'm doing."

"Could you make that any more vague?"

She couldn't tell him Roni was driving her to a travel agency in Hawthorne Springs to check out a lead on Tom Moore. One of his old girlfriends had mentioned the Blue Yonder agency when Sam pretended she needed to find an agent to book her spring vacation. The girl had said she'd picked up tickets for a good friend there once. It could be a dead end, but Sam had to investigate.

Scott raised his hands in mock surrender. "Don't bother to answer. You're working on another NCAA story, aren't you?"

"Yes." She was glad he appreciated the confidentiality that was required: There was no way she could tell him her new subject was one of his teammates. "But if you're going to skip the dining hall tonight, maybe we could get together later."

"And do what?" he asked suggestively.

Sam sighed. "I've got a test in statistics class tomorrow. I was hoping you could quiz me."

He tugged on a length of her hair. "That's just what I was hoping you'd say."

Sam laughed and threw her arms around his waist. She propped her chin on his chest and looked up into his face. "I'm crazy about you, you know."

He bent over for a quick kiss and told Sam she'd better get going before he didn't let her go to her appointment. Sam hurried back to Rogers. Roni was waiting for her in the living room, jingling her car keys impatiently.

"The Blue Yonder closes in forty minutes," she told Sam.

"Then let's get going." Sam already had a small memo pad packed in her purse.

"That's it?" Roni drawled. "You're not going to tell me where you've been all this time? Oh, never mind. I can tell just by looking at you that you've been with Scott."

"You're right!"

"Well, I'm glad you could tear yourself away from that hunk. I hope your friend at the travel agency makes it all worthwhile."

"So do I." Sam hadn't been able to tell Roni why she was visiting the agency, but that didn't bother her suitemate. "If it goes well, dinner's my treat."

"Here's my work for the next *Herald*." Sam mustered a smile and gave Mark her highlight column on Bart Hanson along with her NCAA article on Scott.

"You're certainly in a good mood today," Mark observed. "Aren't you nervous that Scott will be upset about the article?"

"A little. No, a lot. But you said yourself I made a strong defense for his case. I made the corrections you suggested after seeing my draft." Late Friday afternoon, she'd left a copy of her story for him to review. Now she just had to keep telling herself things would be fine.

"It's an excellent article," he assured her. "I wish all the investigations were as thoroughly researched as this one."

"I'm still digging for a few facts on Tom Moore's case. I'm waiting for someone to get back to me on a possible lead," she said.

"If you can keep up the good work, you're going to be a dynamite member of this team."

"Mark!" Sam stood back and stared at him. "Don't get carried away."

"I'm serious," he insisted. "I know it must have been hard for you to do the article on Scott. I had no idea things were going to get so hot and heavy between you two while you were working on the story."

Sam coughed. "Hot and heavy?"

"Sometimes it looks as if you guys are Siamese twins," he told her. "Inseparable."

"I didn't know anyone had noticed." Sam felt a blush rising on her face.

Mark repeated his compliments, saying he knew she'd researched and written the article under a lot of pressure. In return, Sam thanked him for his help. He didn't have any new assignments for her yet, so Sam headed for Scott's dorm.

He had been busy after the game last night, but Sam hadn't minded because she was still working on the story. It would have been hard to face him when she was all wrapped up with the final version of her article. Now that the article was sitting on Mark's desk, Sam planned to forget about it for a while. She wouldn't be able to ignore it on Monday, but she was going to have a good time with Scott until then.

The last time she'd seen Scott, he had invited her to study with him Saturday afternoon. She knocked on his door and didn't hear anything inside his room. Sam knocked again because she was sure he had told her to stop by anytime. Just as she was ready to leave, there were soft footsteps on the other side of the door.

"Scott? It's me," she called.

"I know," he said, opening the door slowly.

Sam blinked as she brushed past him into the

room. The curtains were drawn, throwing shadows across the beds and desks. Scott didn't look much better. He was padding around the floor in stocking feet, and he was wearing an old, ripped T-shirt over a pair of sweat pants. He looked as though he hadn't shaved in the last two days.

"Are you sick?" she asked. "Can I get you something?"

"You might say I'm sick," he said curiously, reaching for a few sheets of paper on his desk. "This was under my door last night when I got back from the game."

She took the papers from him, trying to keep her hands from shaking. It was a photocopy of the first draft of her article on him, the one she'd left for Mark at the *Herald* office yesterday afternoon. Her voice was a hoarse whisper when she asked, "Who gave this to you?"

"I have no idea, but that's not important. I assume everyone's going to read this story in Monday's paper. And I mean, everyone."

Sam didn't know what to say. She thought Scott would be glad that she had cleared his name for good.

"Sam, I thought we trusted each other," he said, making it sound as if he now found the idea ludicrous.

"We did . . . I mean, we do." Sam felt as if she were going to be sick to her stomach. Scott looked so hurt, and so angry.

He paced around the room in front of Sam. "I

suppose it was you who called my bank at home."

"Yes, it was," Sam admitted. Since he had figured out a few things, Sam knew more lies would simply make things worse.

"I won't ask who else you called to reconstruct that one month of my life two years ago." Scott's voice was steady, and controlled. Sam almost wished he would scream at her; she thought she could deal with that better than this complete self-control. Suddenly his mouth dropped open and Sam expected the loud accusations to begin. "I just figured out when you made all those calls . . . the day after you listened to me spill my guts about the pro scouts and my future." The timing seemed to horrify Scott.

"One thing had nothing to do with the other," Sam tried to explain. "I wasn't plotting phone calls while we talked that night! I wasn't thinking about my story at all."

"That night meant so much to me," he whispered, as if thinking aloud. "And I have been so stupid." He sat on the edge of his bed, then rested his elbows on his knees and buried his head in his hands.

Sam's heart ached, as much for his pain as for her own sinking suspicion that she wasn't going to be able to change his mind. "Scott," she began softly, "it had to be done. It's not like I invented the stories about the car. The rumor was all over campus, and Mark insisted it be part of the series." When Scott didn't try to stop her, Sam went on. "I thought I was doing you a favor by proving the rumor was false."

"A favor?" He looked up with total disbelief on his face. Rubbing his stubbly chin, he said, "I didn't do anything wrong. I didn't *need* your favor—my name didn't *need* to be defended."

"Look, Scott, I knew all along you were innocent, but the article still had to be written," she argued. "If I didn't write it, someone else would have."

"Maybe you thought I was innocent and maybe you didn't . . . all I know is you lied to me," he charged, emotion flashing in his eyes for the first time.

"What do you think I should have done?" she inquired.

"Refuse to do the article, tell them it wasn't true," he suggested. "Or couldn't you pass up a hot story like mine?"

"I tried to get out of it, but Mark couldn't give my assignments to anyone else," Sam pleaded. "And I knew I'd work my hardest to defend your reputation."

"Did you ever think of just *telling* me about the rumor, and asking if it was true?" Scott shook his head, as if to say he'd never understand what she'd done.

Sam put her hands on her hips, preparing to deal with Scott's stubborn streak. "You would have told me the story was a lie, I would have told Mark I believed you, and Mark would have laughed me right out of the *Herald* office. He needed proof, Scott."

"Are you sure you did all this sneaking around just to find evidence for Mark Malone?" His tone announced he didn't believe her tidy explanation. "I think you needed a little convincing yourself."

"That's not true!" Sam cried.

"Suit yourself," he said sourly. "I guess you're going to believe you did the right thing, no matter what I say or do."

"And it sounds like you've made up your mind that I did the worst thing in the world, even though I did it because I had to, and because I cared about you." Sam didn't know what else to say. Either Scott believed her, or it was all over between them. She didn't want to think that way, but it was the truth and she had to face it.

"I can't believe I didn't see you for the person you really are. I can't believe I let you fool me!" His intense gaze sent a shiver of dread down Sam's back. "I thought you were an honorable person, and I guess I wanted you to be like that so much that I saw things in you that really weren't there."

Sam was dumbfounded. He was saying everything he'd liked about her didn't exist. It simply wasn't true, but she couldn't find a way to correct him. Words would be hollow and unconvincing. The only thing that might affect him would be her finding a way to keep the story out of Monday's paper, but that was one thing Sam would not do. Besides the unprofessional implications, it would look like she wasn't standing behind her findings; that she'd learned one more thing that convicted Scott of the charges.

"I'm not surprised you can't defend yourself." Scott stood up and walked toward the door. Sam sensed it was her invitation to get lost. "You went behind my back. You betrayed me. I'll never trust you again. And without trust, we have nothing."

Other couples broke up with screaming fights, in which both people expressed their hurt and their anger. But Scott had slickly cut Sam's heart to pieces, and now he was dismissing her. It seemed silly to even say good-bye. He'd made it clear she didn't even exist for him anymore.

She pushed past him and didn't stop moving until she was out of the dorm. It was a warm day for January, and Sam's tears ran freely down her cheeks. How had she gotten in so deep when she hadn't even been looking for a boyfriend? And how had she fallen in love so quickly?

Sam knew there were lessons to be learned. The most obvious was that if something seemed too good to be true, it probably was. She would have plenty of lonely evenings to think about what else she'd learned.

words out of bearable impressiveness tolerable—
none. It was after dark that she was standing
behind the railing that she'd noticed one profile
talking that emended Sam didn't realize . . .

"I'm not sure what you can't defend yourself."
Sam stood and grand walked toward the door. Sam
sensed Sam was just flustered to get out. What was
going on inside you just stayed me till never trust
you again. And we'd just over to have nothing.

Once the guts broke up with something funny,
at which both people expressed within itself and
their hearts. But Sam, she slowly cut down's heart
to pieces, and now she was dismissing her. It
seemed silly to try say good bye. He'd made if
only she didn't even cared for him any more.

She rushed past him and didn't stop until she
until she was out of the dorm. It was a warm day
and somehow Sam's tears ran freely down her
cheeks. How she had she come her deep when she
had, I even been looking for a boyfriend? And
how had she fallen in love so quickly.

Still, for all there were lessons to be learned.
The most obvious was that if something seemed
too good to be true, it probably was. She would
have plenty of lonely evenings to think of all
what else she'd learned.

Sam couldn't drag herself out of bed Sunday morning. Her friends had been wonderful trying to console her last night, but she had been too upset to fully appreciate them. She'd climbed into bed early and pulled the covers over her head.

All night she had tried to understand why she was taking this thing so badly. She had dated Jon for years, and she and Aaron had been talking about getting married. She had only known Scott O'Connor for four weeks. Sure, Scott was the most terrific guy Sam had met since she discovered, in the sixth grade, that boys weren't disgusting creatures, and she couldn't know if she would ever meet anyone else like him; but he hadn't made any commitments to her. And he hadn't listened to her reasons for doing the story. He had really let her down.

Sam had come to respect Scott's opinions in those four weeks, and he had completely taken advantage of that respect. He had insulted her on unjust grounds, implying she had used him, just like the girls who wanted him simply because he was a basketball star. He probably thought she only went out with him in order to dig up information for her assignment, so that *she'd* be the star when her article came out.

Sam knew she hadn't researched and written the article with any selfish purpose in mind. She hadn't worked that hard just to impress Mark or any of the *Herald*'s readers. Her motives had been to meet her obligations to the Hawthorne community and to present Scott's story fairly. Her conscience was clear, but it didn't do her any good if Scott didn't believe that.

The door to Sam's room opened wide, and Maddie walked in with a bouquet of roses. For a second, Sam's heart pounded as she wondered if maybe Scott had sent them as an apology. Then Stacy and Roni came in behind her, carrying a tray.

"We got your favorite," Roni said cheerfully. She pointed to the bakery box next to the coffee carafe on the tray. "Chocolate doughnuts with chocolate frosting."

"Just what I need," she mumbled. "I can eat the whole dozen and lie around getting fat."

"It's not like you to feel sorry for yourself,"

Maddie said, setting the roses on the desk next to Sam's bed.

"I've been dumped once too often in the past year." Sam sighed. Thinking about her rotten romance record made her feel like such a loser. "I deserve this opportunity to lie around and feel sorry for myself."

"This guy really did a job on you, huh?" Maddie broke a piece off a doughnut and popped it into her mouth.

"I didn't know you were in so deep," Roni said. "I made a lot of jokes about your crush on Scott, but when you started going out with him I had no idea you'd get hurt this badly."

"I can't believe he wouldn't listen to me," Sam said, beginning to sort out her wounded feelings. "Last night, I told you what he said about me. He accused me of using our relationship to get a good story. And although I'm totally innocent of his charges, I've been found guilty, without a fair trial."

"You should tell him how you feel. From what you've told us about him before, he wouldn't hurt you this way intentionally. He can't realize what he's done to you." Maddie poured a cup of coffee and handed it to Sam.

Sam sipped the hot coffee, remembering the controlled, measured tone of his voice. Although he was angry, Scott had known exactly what he was saying to her. Nothing had slipped out in a hot, passionate exchange. "Trust me. He said just what he wanted to say yesterday."

"The Sam Hill *we* all know would try to talk to him again," Stacy told her.

"But you don't understand. He won't let me talk to him. I tried to defend myself, and he was deaf to my side of the story. He's made up his mind about me, and he's not going to change it."

"So you're going to give *up*?" Roni made it sound as though Sam would be committing a cardinal sin.

"I don't see it that way. I'm just cutting my losses so I can get on with my life."

"By spending the day in bed?" Maddie inquired.

"No." Sam kicked off her covers and dropped her legs over the side of her bed. "I'm going to finish this cup of coffee, get dressed, and tackle the homework I've let pile up while I got involved with someone who *I* thought was special."

"Don't get bitter," Roni advised. "You had a lot of fun with him while it lasted."

Sam rubbed her eyes and let Roni's comment sink in. "You're right. I'm hurt and disappointed, but nothing so terrible happened that I can't put it behind me and start again. In fact, I should be getting pretty good at recovering from affairs of the heart by now."

"Practice makes perfect," Maddie teased.

Roni pulled a note from her pocket. "Last night, Angie took a message for you. The Blue Yonder travel agency called."

"They did?" Sam reached for the scrap of paper.

"Planning a trip?" Stacy wondered aloud. "Nothing like a few days on a sandy beach to heal the soul."

"That sounds wonderful, but this is a possible lead on one of my stories." Sam hoped the woman at the agency had good news.

Roni checked her watch. "You could call them now."

"I can wait," Sam said delicately. Until she actually made a break in the story, she didn't want anyone to know her next subject was Tom Moore.

"Is it another NCAA scoop?" Maddie wanted to know.

"Yeah. I'm sorry I can't tell you about it yet—"

"Don't apologize to us," Roni insisted. "But I'm amazed you can still think about the paper after the way your work came between you and Scott."

"It's my job," Sam told them all. "I don't feel guilty about doing it, because I know my research is thorough and my stories are fair."

"Too bad Scott was too blind to notice that," Maddie sympathized.

"You're right." Sam shook her head sadly. "My conscience is clear and I'm proud of my work, but my conscience and my pride don't make me as happy as Scott used to. I'm really going to miss him. Oh, well. I'd better get dressed and face the world on my own. It looks like that's the way it's going to be from now on."

"Can I help you?" Sam asked Angie. Her roommate was sorting through stacks of flyers, buttons, and protest signs on her bed.

"Under the circumstances, I hate to ask you to get involved in the demonstration," she replied cautiously.

"Angie, would you please stop treating me like a piece of china? I lost a boyfriend, but it's not the end of the world. I want to help you."

"Really?" Angie sighed with relief. "Good, because I have so much to do before Saturday. There are volunteers coming over to pick up the flyers. I still want to get more of the buttons in circulation. And I've got an interview with an animal-protection newsletter person in half an hour."

"I thought the flyers were already posted around campus," Sam said, hoping she could help Angie get organized.

"They were, but someone's been tearing them down. The volunteers are going to tack these new copies up wherever they see an empty space."

"Could I do something with the buttons?" Sam inquired.

"Tucker has convinced the bookstore to keep a basket of them on the check-out counter. I was supposed to deliver a supply this afternoon, but I'm not exactly sure when this reporter is going to show up." Angie ran her hand through her long, red-gold hair. Her cheeks were flushed with excitement and nervous energy.

"I can take them over to the bookstore," Sam offered.

"That would be a lifesaver," Angie sighed. "We just have to put three hundred of them in this box. I've already got them bundled in plastic sacks of fifty each."

"You really are organized." Sam was impressed. By the time Angie was a senior, the campus was likely to be a whole different place if she continued her efforts to raise student consciousness.

"Thanks. I want news of the protest to be all over the campus when the TV crews arrive," she explained.

"TV crews?"

"Didn't you know?" Angie looked up from her bags of buttons. "Someone in Atlanta saw the article in the *Herald* and a television news crew wants to cover it—unless some other news story breaks on Saturday."

"That's super." Sam was happy for Angie; it felt good to see things working out for her roommate, especially after the problems she'd had with her last organized project.

Sam's own life had been bumpy since Saturday afternoon last week. She'd made it to all her classes, caught up on her homework, and discovered someone other than Tom had paid Blue Yonder for his plane tickets. Her dedication to the *Herald* had started to pay off: Mark had told her Eddie Sawyer, the editor-in-chief, liked her work on the NCAA series. But it had been incredibly hard for Sam to see Scott in the dining hall and ignore him. She was surviving, but Sam would be glad when the first week without him was over. Things always got easier with time.

When the alarm rang at seven o'clock on Saturday morning, Angie crawled out of bed and peeked through the curtains. "Oh no! It looks like it's going to start raining any minute."

Sam yawned and tried to figure out why Angie cared about the weather. Then she remembered the demonstration. "Oh no is right—it can't rain!"

Two hours later, the group from Rogers House joined the picket line in front of the psych building. Unfortunately, everyone was holding umbrellas instead of protest signs.

"Why are we here?" Roni asked, the rain sliding down the folds of her yellow slicker. The girls were clustered near the back of the crowd, hoping to get some protection from the building's ledge. In front of them, Angie was finishing her opening comments and introducing the next speaker.

"I guess we're here to save the monkeys," Maddie answered from beneath her oversized yellow-and-green umbrella.

"I thought Sam woke us all up this morning because we're doing this for Angie." Stacy had covered her wool sweater and pants with a plaid waterproof cape that fell below her knees.

"Are you sure we're not here to soak up moisture and pamper our complexions?" Roni suggested.

"You do that in a sauna, don't you?" Maddie

asked. "It's too cold out here for the moisture to soak in and do any good."

Sam looked from one girl to the next. "Don't you know why we're standing around in the rain?"

"I suppose you're going to tell us," Roni drawled.

"We're always around for each other. Just think of what you did to help me get over Aaron last summer," Sam told them. "Not to mention holding my hand all weekend after Scott blew me off."

"You sure helped me survive my summer fiasco with Carter Cabot. I couldn't believe I'd let a graduate student talk me into stealing papers for him." Stacy shook her head. "It was great knowing I could count on you guys."

"And you listened to my complaints about Erica," Maddie added. "You probably kept me sane."

"What about me?" Roni scooted closer to the others. "I wouldn't have passed biology in summer school without all of you helping me."

"That's a fact!" Stacy exclaimed with a broad grin on her face.

"You're right, Sam. We do depend on one another a lot," Maddie said, summing up the conversation. "But why are we all standing in the rain for Angie?"

Sam bit her lower lip, trying to come up with an answer. "I guess I'm here because she's my roommate and I admire her for doing this kind of thing. I suppose the rest of you are here to make sure I don't freeze to death or get trampled if the demonstration turns violent. I don't exactly have a good history when it comes to demonstrations," she added.

"I might have come even if you'd stayed in bed, Sam," Maddie announced. "I really admire Angie, too."

Roni pressed a hand to her forehead. "Let's not get carried away. If you're going to take Angie into the group, she'll make us start drinking decaffeinated coffee."

They moaned in unison and decided they'd stand in the rain for Angie, but giving up coffee was out of the question. Their friendship had made it through some hard times, but the group couldn't survive without their morning coffee together.

"Did you talk to Mark Malone when you turned in your athlete-of-the-week article last night?" Stacy asked.

"Yeah. He still hasn't found out who copied that article and slipped it under Scott's door."

"Are you sure he didn't do it himself?" Roni queried. "He sounds like such a jerk."

"It wasn't him," Sam said with certainty. She had earned Mark's respect with the article on Scott. He felt responsible for the breakup because someone had taken the draft off his desk.

"Look! It's Erica!" Maddie exclaimed. The freshman was an eyeful in her coordinated umbrella, raincoat, and plastic rain boots.

"What's she doing out here?" Roni asked with an unbelieving giggle. "Isn't she afraid her mascara will run?"

"Ooh . . . I bet I know," Maddie announced. "Last night Liz and Angie were visiting Jean, and Angie mentioned the magic words that caught Erica's attention—*TV crew*! Her head snapped up so fast that I thought she'd get whiplash."

"But it's only a news crew—if they even bother to show up on a day like this," Sam told them.

Roni pressed a finger to her lips, a wicked gleam in her eye. "Let's not tell her."

All of sudden, Sam sensed someone had walked up behind her. She turned around and saw a green sleeve that looked like part of a Hawthorne letter jacket. Squinting her eyes to keep the rain out of them, she looked up.

"Scott?"

"Would you like to share with me?" he asked, inviting her to step under his huge umbrella.

"I don't know." If Scott wanted Sam to step under his umbrella so he could insult her some more, she would rather skip the extra misery.

He grabbed her arm and she glared up at him. "I'm sorry, Sam," he said softly. "Can I talk to you for a few minutes?" he asked. "Please?"

He sounded too nice for Sam to think that he was planning to insult her again. She decided to give him a chance. Besides, his umbrella looked stronger than hers. She lowered her umbrella and shook it out before taking two steps toward Scott.

"Sam, I was wrong," he said humbly.

Sam shouldn't have been surprised, but she was. If she had thought about how Scott might apologize, she would have realized he would be direct and honest. Her automatic reaction was to tell him everything was all right, but it wasn't. She held her tongue.

Angie was on the podium again, leading the demonstrators in a chant. Sam noticed her friends had joined the rest of the crowd; she could hear Roni shouting at the top of her lungs.

Scott leaned close to her so she could hear him in the midst of the noise. "I was really upset about the article."

"I could tell," she said wryly.

"I'd never even *heard* that rumor. It hurt me that when you did, you ran off to write an article about it without warning me."

"Do you think I liked keeping it from you?" Sam finally felt as if she had a chance to reason with him. It had taken him a week, but he seemed ready to listen.

"You don't have to defend yourself, Sam," he said gently. "I know that people sometimes have to do things they don't want to do. I figured out that this was like the time I twisted my ankle in a game and Coach Tupper wouldn't let me keep playing. I had to do as I was told for the good of the team. I don't know why it took me so long to see that you feel the same way about the paper as I do about the basketball team. I should have understood you have to play by their rules."

"So you can live with the article and the fact that I wrote it?" Sam wanted to make sure she wasn't reading anything into his comments.

"I was dreading last Monday, but instead of feeling victimized when the paper came out, I felt proud. People who had assumed I was guilty came up and apologized for believing the rumor. I have to admit, you wrote a great article."

"Thanks." Sam was confused. He seemed to understand why she hadn't told him she was working on the assignment. And it sounded like he'd finally read the article with some objectivity, and that he appreciated all she'd done to back up his story. Where did that leave them? She glanced into Scott's eyes. He looked as confused as she felt.

"I'm asking if we can forget what happened Saturday." He stared at the ground, waiting for her response.

"Some of the things you said really hurt me, Scott." Sam wasn't trying to make him suffer, but the things he'd said to her that day weren't going to disappear at the snap of a finger. "I'm not the kind of person who deliberately uses people and cheats on them. You implied I was like that, and worse."

He stared at the raindrops splashing in the puddle at his feet. "I guess when I said the trust between us was broken, it went both ways."

"I guess it did," Sam agreed.

Scott cleared his throat nervously. "If I were to admit I should have trusted you, do you think you could find a way to see me again?"

"Are you saying you could trust me if we . . . got back together?" Sam closed her eyes and hoped she hadn't made a fool of herself by suggesting he might want her back.

"Sam," he said impatiently, "I'm trying to ask you to give me another chance."

"You are?"

"I overreacted to the article. I said stupid things on Saturday afternoon. I've missed you like crazy ever since."

"Then why did you wait so long to find me?" Sam moved closer to him.

He put his arm around her and hugged her against his side. "I was afraid," he confessed.

"Afraid?" Fear was not an emotion Sam associated with Scott.

"Afraid you hated me. Afraid I'd driven you away forever. Afraid you wouldn't take me back . . ." He smiled. "The list is endless."

"I think you should have been afraid of just one thing," she said. "That you're going to be stuck with me for a long time."

He scooped her into his arms, and both their umbrellas fell to the ground. Sam wrapped her arms around his neck and her mouth met his in a joyous kiss as the rain fell on them. Sam had been right all along—Scott was the perfect guy for her. And she wasn't about to let him go.

Here's a sneak preview of *Model Student*, book number thirteen in the continuing ROOMMATES series from Ivy Books.

Erica hurried across the student-filled quad, feeling as though she had been let out of jail. What bliss to be away from Rogers House! A sore throat had kept her home in bed for the last two days, so she had been a captive audience as people came in and out of the suite congratulating Stacy on landing the modeling assignment as the McLean's girl.

Naturally everyone seemed to want to hear all the details, and Erica was sure if she had to listen once more to Stacy replay the fateful moment when Mr. Galvin came out of his office offering her the job, she would have screamed, sore throat and all.

To add insult to injury, Erica's own career plans seemed to be going nowhere. She had missed her first class with Robert Egan and she hadn't even been able to follow through on her plan to discover where he lived or how he spent his free time. *Boy*, Erica thought with disgust, *why does everything always have to happen to me?* At least today's improv session would give her the opportunity to make Egan notice her—and Erica intended to make the most of it.

Glancing at her watch, Erica wondered if she had time for a soda at the Student Union before the workshop got underway. She decided to risk it. Her throat was still dry and painful, and besides, she didn't want to be the first one in the auditorium. That would be too obvious.

As she walked in the door, Erica saw Kitty sitting in the corner of the large cafeteria. Erica bought a soda and then slid into a seat across from her friend.

"Erica," Kitty said, looking up from her poetry book. "Long time no see."

"Well, if you were really my friend, you would have realized that I've been sick."

"Hey, I was in bed for a week last fall and you didn't even call me until I was better," Kitty protested.

"Maybe," Erica admitted, "but you weren't forced to listen to the saga of Stacy Swanson while you tried to recuperate."

Kitty's expression grew more animated. "I've been wanting to hear about Stacy's job! It's all over campus. Do you think she'll get on the cover of *Glamour*?"

"Not you, too!" Erica cried. "I'm so sick of hearing the name Stacy I could spit. So she got one little assignment. Big deal."

"Erica, you've got to admit it's more than just an assignment. This could be a really big break for Stacy."

Erica let out a loud sigh. "I don't want to hear about it. What about me, for goodness sakes?"

"What about you?" Kitty asked.

"I'm the one who's going to be a famous actress." *Fools and idiots*, Erica thought heatedly. *I'm surrounded by them.*

Kitty smiled. "Maybe someday, but right now you're a famous actress who doesn't have a job. Stacy does."

"Fine," Erica snapped, pushing her chair back from the table to stand up. "But I'm going to go get one. And when I do, I sure won't tell you about it!"

Have you been wondering what those
Lewis girls are up to?

SISTERS Returns in August!

The last time we saw the Lewis sisters was during their summer vacation in Quebec. But beginning this August, Nicole will leave the nest as the *Sisters* series continues in COLLEGE BOUND by Jennifer Cole.

Will 16-year-old Cindy reunite with Grant after their long summer apart?

Will younger sister Mollie keep in touch with her new first love, Paul?

Will Nicole keep up her grades while enjoying her new life in a college dorm?

Look for Fawcett Girls Only's thirteenth *Sisters* novel, COLLEGE BOUND, in August wherever paperbacks are sold. Or use this coupon to order by mail.

JOB-2